AN AIR OF MURDER

AN AIR OF MURDER

Roderic Jeffries

Severn House Large Print
London & New York

This first large print edition published in Great Britain 2006 by
SEVERN HOUSE LARGE PRINT BOOKS LTD of
9-15 High Street, Sutton, Surrey, SM1 1DF.
First world regular print edition published 2003 by
Severn House Publishers, London and New York.
This first large print edition published in the USA 2006 by
SEVERN HOUSE PUBLISHERS INC., of
595 Madison Avenue, New York, NY 10022.

British Library Cataloguing in Publication Data

Jeffries, Roderic, 1926-
    An air of murder. - Large print ed.
    1. Alvarez, Enrique (Fictitious character) - Fiction
    2. Police - Spain - Majorca - Fiction
    3. Majorca (Spain) - Fiction
    4. Detective and mystery stories
    5. Large type books
    I. Title
    823.9'14 [F]

    ISBN-10: 0-7278-7495-0

Printed and bound in Great Britain by
MPG Books Ltd, Bodmin, Cornwall.

One

As Laura turned to face her husband, her dark glasses glinted in the sunlight passing through the overhead vine leaves. 'When does Heloise's plane arrive?'

'Half five,' Gerrard answered.

'Since she was so rude, ordering you to meet her, why on earth didn't you say you'd be too busy and she'd have to take a taxi from the airport?'

'Now that I think about it, I've no idea why I didn't.'

'Liar!'

He smiled.

'You know damn well it's because you can't stop behaving like a gentleman.'

'It's because she's my sister-in-law.'

'A cross to bear which you should have lightened.'

'My sweet, you are beginning to sound a trifle sour.'

'Knowing she's arriving makes me feel sourer than an unripe caqui.'

'Which is what?'

'You must know.'

'Would I ask if I did?'

'Ralph said the other day that the average Englishman who lives here only ever learns four Spanish words – vino rojo, rosado, and blanco.'

'We Brits concentrate on essentials.'

'Have I ever told you, your sense of humour is becoming flaccid?'

'Many times, and after I looked the word up in a dictionary, I understood what you were getting at.'

'Give me patience! ... I wonder if Heloise will arrive looking as if she's about to start work in Soho?'

'Is one allowed to hope?'

'You are becoming irritating.'

'Even after many years of marriage, a good husband tries to entertain his wife.'

'Then could you do so less facetiously?' She drew her colourful linen skirt further up her thighs. 'God! It's hot and we're only in May. What's it going to be in July and August?'

'Baking.'

'If Heloise doesn't stay for long, we can spend the days in her pool.'

'We can, whatever. She's always told us to enjoy it as if it were our own.'

'And if we take advantage of the offer, she'll give us reason to regret we have.'

'Meow!'

She was silent for a moment, then said: 'Small wonder Jerome wasn't happy with her.'

'What on earth draws you to that conclusion?'

'Mainly female intuition.'

'Notoriously capricious.'

'Perhaps he'd begun to suspect that when being chairman of that agricultural trust took him abroad, she was entertained by someone else.'

'That's ridiculous.'

'Is it? She wasn't made for constancy, and she's so self-centred, she'd have believed she could always fool him because of his trust in her.'

'You've more reason than female intuition for talking like this, haven't you?'

'In a way.'

'In what way?'

'There was a whisper that at least once when Jerome went abroad, she wasn't as lonely as she should have been.'

'Who was doing the whispering? Miranda? Her tongue would destroy a saint's reputation in seconds.'

'It wasn't she.'

He picked up a glass and drained it. 'If there's any truth in the suggestion, one could say he was fortunate to die when he did.'

'Very true. He'd have been emotionally shattered to learn she'd been cuckolding him; he never really understood how much the world had changed and that most of what he believed in had become derided. He was a refugee from the time when honour and patriotism weren't guaranteed laughs for comedians. Stayforth House, its contents, the land, meant so much more to him than just possessions; the estate was a part of history for which he'd become a guardian, and if she'd betrayed him, she'd have destroyed his guardianship. I'm probably not talking sense, but you'll understand what I mean. You see things as he did.'

'I'm not certain of that.'

'Only because you don't like admitting to the emotional tie there is between you and Stayforth. Look how upset you were to hear she'd persuaded the trustees to sell one of the Van Dycks.'

'Surprised is the word I'd have used.'

'So surprised, you swore you'd take the trustees to court for agreeing to the sale.'

'But better counsel very quickly prevailed when I accepted that they'd judged money had to be found for repairs and the sale of one of the paintings was the sensible way of finding it.'

'Provided none of the money funds her luxury suite on the latest must-do cruise liner or a month in the Bahamas.'

'The trustees will make certain it doesn't.'

'You underrate her wiles.'

'You're really damning her!'

'She makes a better job of doing that than ever I can.' She was silent for several seconds, then said, rather diffidently: 'Aren't there times when you feel really bitter that someone like she should live in Stayforth and it's Fergus's?'

'Sad, not bitter. Don't forget that from the moment I could appreciate such things, I learned that in order to maintain estates and prevent their being broken up, they always passed through to the eldest son. I knew Jerome and then his son would get every-thing.'

'It's so damned unfair.'

'But effective, as witness the many historic estates which still survive and are one of the glories of our country.'

'Dale was quite right.'

'What exactly has our son been saying now?'

'You are way behind the twenty-first

9

century.'

'It's not often one receives so generous an encomium from one's son.'

'I don't have to point out that that is not what was intended.'

'What son worth his salt ever praises his father?' He stood. 'Basil told me his infallible way of identifying a newcomer to the island – he sits in front of an empty glass. Pass me yours and I'll refill it.'

She handed it to him.

He went indoors. Ca'n Dento was bereft of any suggestion of architectural grace, having been built a century and a half before, for staff who worked in the manor house. Although modernised to a basic level, it now offered a far better quality of life than any of the previous inhabitants had ever known or even envisaged. The front door led directly into the small sitting-room; one had to go through the kitchen to reach the bathroom or the patio; the two upstairs bedrooms could have been regularly shaped, but weren't because part of one of them had been extended into the other in a narrow rectangle for an inexplicable reason. When Jerome had bought the big house – then called Ca'n Plomo – Ca'n Dento had been uninhabited for many years and become little more than a ruin.

The kitchen was the largest room since it was there a family would have spent most of their free waking time. The ceiling was beamed and in the beams were the hooks from which strings of garlic, onions, tomatoes, botifarró, chorizo, and sobrasada had once hung; the open fireplace was very large and on either side were narrow recessed seats in which people had sought what warmth they could from the wood fire when the winter winds brought cold, wet and, once in thirty or forty years, snow.

He opened one of the cupboards, brought out a bottle of gin, poured two drinks, filled the glasses with iced tonic from the refrigerator. He carried the glasses out onto the narrow patio which enjoyed the shade of the overhead vine from which hung bunches of grapes, still little more than berries.

He put one glass down in front of her on the glass-topped bamboo table, sat. He stared out at the garden – this more in name than fact because the ground was poor, stony, and already too hard to work – at the backdrop of mountains, part of the chain which ran the length of the island, and finally at the many roofs of Heloise's house visible above pine trees. Ca'n Plomo had been owned by a wealthy family of known politically left-wing sympathies. The Civil

War had forced them to flee the island and cost the lives of father and eldest son, and all their wealth. After the war had ended, the house had remained uninhabited, even though there were many who would have welcomed its shelter, because of the political taint they irrationally feared would result in their occupying it. When the tourist invasion began, the property had been put up for sale and an Englishman, escaping from tax officials who found great difficulty in believing that a man living in great luxury was earning no more than a reasonably inefficient plumber, had bought it, had the old manor house knocked down and in its place a large, modern house built. Only remedial work had been carried out on Ca'n Dento since he believed that to provide staff with even a hint of comfort was to pander to their innate laziness. Jerome had purchased the property from him and Heloise had demanded the name be changed to Ca'n Jerome...

'Where have you disappeared to?' Laura asked.

'I was remembering how Heloise decided their place had to be renamed because she'd learned houses were often called by nicknames and Plomo meant lead. Whoever told her failed to point out the fact that in this

12

instance, Plomo ironically suggested the owner of the house was wealthy.'

'Even if she'd learned that, I doubt she'd have understood.'

'Probably not. Most females find difficulty in appreciating irony.'

'Being far too straightforward ... I suppose there's room for surprise she didn't want it called Ca'n Sir Jerome.'

He chuckled.

'I wish...' She stopped.

'Wish what?'

'That you didn't just laugh.'

'Humour is said to be the best antidote to life's problems.'

'You'll laugh when Fergus comes of age and people have one more reason for damning so-called privilege?'

'It's hardly fair to judge from his present form what he'll be like when that happens.'

'It may not be fair, but only because it's backing a dead cert ... What a fool Jerome was!'

'That's rough.'

'Are you suggesting his marrying Heloise was the act of a wise man?'

The act of a man, he thought, who had left himself totally vulnerable because he had dedicated himself to the saving of the estate. When their parents had died in a plane crash, Jerome, then twenty-one, and he, eighteen and about to enter university, had been shocked to discover how serious were the financial problems of the estate. Jerome, who possessed the faculty of being able to tackle a problem with exhaustive and exhausting tenacity, had worked with the trustees day after day, week after week, month after month to restore financial health. He had finally succeeded, in spite of governments who abhorred the trappings of privilege except for themselves and who refused to understand the benefits of maintaining the countryside, but success had come at the cost of never having had the time to learn that all work and no play not only made for dullness, it also left one unable to judge the quality of the pleasures of life. Ignorance, not stupidity, had been responsible for his marriage.

Gerrard arrived back at Ca'n Dento as the setting sun neared the mountain ridges and the sky gained the mauve tint which marked the end of a hot day. As he drove into the garage – originally a pig-sty – Laura opened the front door and stepped outside. When he approached her, she said: 'I was beginning to worry.'

'I'm sorry, but the plane was late, the

baggage handlers were having their fourth or fortieth merienda of the day, and when I tried to use the mobile to warn you I'd be late back, the battery was flat.'

'I did remind you to put it on charge.'

'You did. But after the age of thirty, one's memory cells vanish like snow flakes in the Sahara.'

'Which was why you forgot you could use one of the public phones?'

'Spanish efficiency kept me dashing from one end of the arrival hall to the other as they three times changed the gate at which the passengers would come through because a carousel broke down and I knew that if she didn't find me waiting to carry her bags, she'd be bitching harder than ever. And when there was a pause in my frenzied perambulations and I tried to use a pay phone, it was always to find them all occupied by garrulous females or out of order.'

'Over-detailed explanations never sound wholly convincing.'

'You're calling me a liar?'

'Ten to one, because you had time to wait, your mind drifted to that other universe it seems to inhabit part of the time and it just never occurred to you I might start worrying if you weren't back in a reasonable time and there'd been no word from you.'

'Since confession is said to be good for the soul, I'll admit, you're right. It was only after I'd met her ladyship, listened to her criticisms concerning her fellow passengers, escorted her to our ancient car, suffered her complaints at the discomfort of the front passenger seat, meekly accepted her criticisms of my driving, and we were approaching the autoroute, I realised just how overdue I'd be and I should warn you. But as I said, the mobile battery is flat.'

'It didn't occur to you to ask to use her mobile?'

'Would it have worked here?'

'Of course it would, since she'll have the most expensive money can buy.'

'Mea culpa.'

'I'll forgive you, being a weak and feeble woman.'

'With the heart and stomach of a king.'

'Thank you very much, my stomach is not the size of a king's.'

'The heart and will of a king.' He kissed her. The degree to which she had been worrying was obvious when she briefly gripped his right arm very firmly.

She released him. 'Let's go in and you can tell me how Heloise is in addition to being bitchy.'

They went through the sitting-room and

16

kitchen out on to the patio, the overhead vine now offering little protection from the low sun. 'What would you like to drink?' he asked.

'A G and T, very long, very cold.'

He returned to the kitchen, poured out two gin and tonics, added ice, carried out the glasses and sat.

'Well?' she said. 'How is she?'

'Where shall I start?'

'With what she was wearing.'

'The Rokeburt pearls and that clasp supposedly made up from diamonds and rubies pinched from a maharaja's palace by one of our ancestors.'

'No clothes? She must have attracted enough attention to satisfy even her ego.'

'She had on a green frock.'

'Describe it.'

'Not much of it.'

'But very chic?'

'Where does chic end and lubricity begin?'

'In a man's mind ... In other words, as tartish as ever?'

'A catty description, but fair.'

'Did she mention what's happened to Fergus after she pulled him out of Barnsford Close because she doesn't believe in sending a son to boarding school and depriving him of his mother's love and affection?'

'He's now at a school I haven't heard of in Middleton.'

'But isn't that Sussex?'

'West Sussex.'

'She's on a school run of a couple of hours twice a day?'

'He's a boarder.'

'But...?'

'After Jerome died and she pulled Fergus out of Barnsford Close, she put him in that prep school less than ten miles from Stayforth. One term was long enough for her to discover the pleasures of enjoying her son's company every day, ferrying him to parties, and the school run, were not for her.'

'How typical! ... That's surely not the prep school which suffered a scandal which almost forced it to close down?'

'The same.'

'Doesn't the woman ever consider anyone but herself?'

'How would she find the time to do that?'

She drank. When she next spoke, her tone was reflective. 'Mind you, I can understand how she felt initially – if she was being genuine – when she tried to persuade Jerome not to send Fergus to Barnsford Close. I remember how I so hated the thought of sending Dale there. It feels almost as if one's rejecting one's child by having strangers look after him through his most formative years.'

'But like her, you retreated in the face of tradition?'

'No. If my doubts had been motivated by more than emotion, he would not have gone to Barnsford. But if I was honest, I have to admit there was so much to be gained; more than he would lose by not being at home. That sense of independence boarding school instils is worth the heartaches.'

'Even the heartache when you can't see him on exeat days; can't even fly him out here very often since I can't make enough money to do more than keep us ticking over?'

'Cut that out, Charles,' she said sharply.

'Cut out the truth?'

'The truth is, you make enough at doing what you want to do to provide a life which offers me all I want.'

He fiddled with his glass, turning it round with thumb and forefinger. 'But that isn't exactly the whole truth, is it? Thanks to Jerome, we live in this house rent free and the trust pays Dale's school fees.'

'Little enough in the circumstances.'

'But if my books were more successful...'

'Success in the arts is a matter of luck as much as ability and you've never had much luck. Your books are good.'

'Modesty forbids my admiring the breadth and depth of your criticism.'

'Why does praise always disturb you?'

'I don't know that it does.'

'If it didn't, you wouldn't indulge in so much self-deprecation.'

'Blame that on my editor, who proffers hope uneasily.'

'Bill ought to do a lot more for you.'

'As a matter of fact, I asked him relatively recently if he could suggest some way in which I could increase sales. He suggested sex. But when I added some in my last script, he pulled it out because it didn't read as if I knew what I was talking about.'

She emptied her glass. 'That's a load of bull. If he would give your books some publicity, they'd sell like hot cakes.'

'Publicity is only offered to books which are selling sufficiently well to pay for the publicity.'

'Then how the hell does one get them selling well initially?'

'One acquires the experience necessary to write authoritatively about lesser-known sexual pleasures.'

'Give me something to throw at you.'

'I'll get more drinks instead.'

Two

Steps in the stone wall provided access to the garden of Ca'n Jerome. As Gerrard climbed the last of these and stepped on to the ground, Laura said: 'Look at the garden!'

Thanks to a well which had never been known to run dry, the lawn was green although elsewhere grass was turning brown because there had been little rain for several weeks, the flower beds were filled with colour, and the six jacaranda trees were in bloom, as was the lantana hedge around the large kidney-shaped swimming pool. 'Emilio must have been working really hard,' she said.

'Having watched him from time to time, that seems unlikely,' he observed. 'Still, to give him his due, it's not every local willing to put effort into growing something that can't be eaten.'

They crossed the lawn to the large house, on the south side of which was an arched and pillared patio that provided a sense of grace it otherwise lacked.

Heloise, wearing a bikini, lay on a chaise longue in the sunshine which reached under the patio roof.

'Morning,' Laura called out as they approached.

Heloise started, opened her eyes, sat upright. 'You startled me, because I wasn't expecting you.' Her tone was resentful.

'I'm sorry, I thought you said one o'clock?'

'I didn't expect you to arrive at the back.'

'No damage done,' Gerrard said, 'since, sadly, you are decent.'

'Shut up!' Laura murmured. 'You know she's no sense of humour.'

'Visitors usually come to the front door,' Heloise observed tartly.

'We're claiming FHB rights,' Gerrard said.

'I don't understand.'

'Family harrives at the back.'

'I apologise for Charles,' Laura said. 'He's in one of his more facetious moods.'

'Obviously.' Heloise stood.

She had everything, Laura thought despondently. Naturally blonde hair with a rippling wave no artifice could match, lapis lazuli eyes, full, shapely lips, a swan neck, a slim body with all the right curves, and the ability to project an innocent sexiness. Small wonder Jerome had not remembered that a cover concealed rather than enhanced the contents.

'I'll change before we have aperitifs ... I'm so glad you haven't dressed up, Laura, because that means I don't have to; so much more fun being casual. Shan't be a moment.' She went inside.

'Must you leer?' Laura demanded.

'She moves her buttocks with sinuous grace,' Gerrard answered.

'So do horses ... My God, I could crown her with an axe!'

'Such jealousy because I enjoy a brief moment of visual pleasure?'

'Don't flatter yourself. I'm mad because she told me I looked like a peasant.'

'I didn't hear her say any such thing.'

'Of course you didn't, being interested in flesh, not words ... Not dressed up, when I put on the smartest frock I have!'

'And look stunning in it.'

'More like a refugee when she returns, flaunting a little something by Galliano.'

Heloise was indeed wearing a dress that had to bear an out-of-sight designer's label. She sat on one of the four chairs grouped around a small table in front of the chaise longue. 'Tell me what you'd like to drink and Filipe can get it.'

'Filipe?' Gerrard queried.

'He and Ana started work here a few days ago – Emilio was supposed to supervise them moving into the servants' quarters, but I don't suppose he did. They were recommended by Georgina, who employed them until she and Robert decided to move to Canada; said they were reasonable workers for Mallorquins ... You know them, I suppose?'

'Filipe and Ana – I don't think we do.'

'Robert and Georgina,' she corrected sharply.

'I sometimes had a brief chat with him when we met, collecting mail at the post office, but I don't suppose I spoke once a month with the duchess. She was out of our financial league.'

'Bernard's not a duke – he doesn't have any title.'

'Duchess was Georgina's nickname, a tribute to her insatiable desire to interfere in other people's lives.'

'Some thought she could be a little over-bearing at times,' Laura hurriedly said, trying to lessen her husband's criticism. 'I've been so looking forward to hearing how Fergus is getting on at his new school, do tell us.'

'I will, after you've said what you'll drink. I can offer anything but champagne. Stupidly, I didn't order more when I was last here and there are only two bottles left; the Fabers are coming to dinner and he won't drink cava – says it's so Spanish.'

'Hugh is a very observant man,' Gerrard observed.

'May I have a gin and tonic?' Laura asked hurriedly. 'I reckon that's the most refreshing drink in this weather.'

'And the same for me, please,' he said.

Heloise made her way into the house.

Laura spoke in a low voice. 'Will you stop being rude.'

'Fighting fire with fire.'

'You're a guest, not a bloody fireman.'

Filipe, hands in white gloves, handed round the plates on each of which were three slices of smoked salmon, a wedge of lemon, and buttered brown bread.

'I'm afraid it's only Norwegian,' Heloise said. 'It seems impossible to buy Scotch here.'

'I'm sure this will be just as delicious,' Laura said politely.

Heloise picked up the wedge of lemon on her plate and squeezed it over the salmon. 'Charles, will you pass the pepper.'

He handed her the wooden mill. As she twisted a fine spray of pepper, she said: 'I asked you here at such short notice because there are one or two things I need to say and I find I'm already very booked up from tomorrow. It really is extraordinary what a busy social life one leads on the island, isn't it?'

'We tend to lead rather a quiet one,' Laura observed.

'That's probably very wise. There is such a mixture of people who live here or come on holiday, one does have to be so careful. In my case, of course, extra-careful.'

'Why's that?' he asked.

'My position.'

'It makes you a target?'

'People seem rather eager to meet me.'

'What more natural?'

'I meant, because of my position.'

'I thought the social kudos of a title had tended to wither in our age of equality?'

'I know it doesn't really mean anything now, and maybe never really did, but some people still do seem to think it adds a certain cachet. Of course, as I've always told everyone, title or no title, we are all the same these days.'

'Unless we're politicians.'

'You think they're better than us?'

'They also are in the gutter, but are incapable of looking up at the stars.'

'You do sometimes say rather odd things.'

'Not sometimes, Heloise, all the time,' Laura corrected.

'I suppose that's why he writes. I tell everyone they must try to read your books, Charles.'

'One hopes they find the attempt not too exhausting. Or perhaps it is only the quest to find one which is difficult?'

'I don't quite ... Where is Filipe? He hasn't poured the wine or put out the bell-push. It's on the sideboard where he must have left it. Plugs in to the right of the sideboard and I like it by my right foot.'

Accepting her words as an indirect command, he stood, crossed to the Regency mahogany sideboard which had come from Stayforth, with or without the trustees' knowledge, inserted the plug and set the bell-push down on the ground by her left foot in a juvenile display of contrariness.

'I explained very clearly what he was to do,' she said, as she used her foot to slide the bell-push along the marble floor. 'Of course, he forgot, as he always does. They are the most feckless people.'

'Did you tell him in Spanish?'

'Of course not.'

'Then perhaps he didn't understand you.'

'Are you suggesting I don't speak good English?'

'Perish the thought. Merely making the point that he may not know the language as well as you think he does.'

'Georgina said he was fluent.'

'Perhaps she was judging by her own standards. Or it was to make you keener to employ him and Ana who, presumably, is his wife?'

'I doubt it. The natives are so immoral.'

The door opened and Filipe entered, came to a stop a metre from where Heloise sat at the head of the table, his sharply featured, dark-toned face expressing uncertainty. 'Señora?'

'Lady Gerrard,' she snapped. 'How many more times do I have to remind you?'

'Please pardon.'

'You didn't put the bell-push by my chair and you haven't poured the wine.'

'I sorry...'

'Get on with it.'

Filipe lifted the bottle out of the wine cooler, wrapped a serviette around it, crossed to where Gerrard sat and prepared to pour.

'For Heaven's sake! You serve the ladies first,' Heloise said angrily.

Filipe went round to Laura's side, filled one of the glasses in front of her.

'They are so stupid,' Heloise said, 'but I suppose one shouldn't be surprised since they're only peasants.'

Filipe served her with wine.

'Are peasants invariably stupid?' Gerrard asked.

'Of course.'

'I wonder. They may have led peasants' lives before the tourists arrived, but since then many have built up very successful businesses; one doesn't do that if one's stupid.'

'They become rich by swindling the foreigners.'

'Who logically have to be less smart than those who swindle them?'

Laura regarded her husband with a shut-up look, then said to Heloise: 'You were going to say how Fergus is getting on at his new school.' She breathed a silent sigh of relief when Heloise did so, knowing her husband would become too bored to offer any comments.

Some twenty-five minutes later, when they had finished the open mixed-fruit tart topped with whipped cream, Heloise said: 'I asked you here because I wanted a word.'

Glad to know it wasn't for our company,

Gerrard silently commented.

'The trustees have become very difficult. When I told them I needed a better income, they said they didn't think that would be possible because the investments were giving a poor return, farm rents were low, and Stayforth House and several of the estate cottages needed repairs. I told them that if money was short, they must sell one of the paintings. There was a ridiculous amount of havering, but in the end they agreed to get rid of one. Then, when I told them how much more they must give me, they refused because the money from the painting had to be treated as capital. I pointed out that they weren't now going to have to use estate income on the buildings so they must be able to give me more, but they said they were under an obligation not to use any more capital than they had to, so they couldn't increase my income by more than a derisory amount. Naturally, I told my solicitor to knock some sense into them, but he was completely useless; claimed he couldn't do anything because the terms of the trust were drawn up so tightly.'

'To make certain the estate survived,' he observed.

'And never mind I'm left damn near penniless? With the cost of living going up every day, I simply have to have more money and since they won't provide it, I'm having to make economies.'

'That shouldn't prove too difficult. To start with, the gardens are large, elaborate, and labour-intensive. There'd be considerable saving if they were simplified and reduced in size.'

'I open them to the public in aid of charity.'

'I know, but...'

'I regard that as a social obligation.'

Performed in the light of self-promotion. 'Another possibility is that the home farm could probably be run more economically. I presume Abbott is still head shepherd?'

'I've no idea.'

'He's a very keen breeder and used to show whenever he could. Does he still run Romney Marsh sheep?'

'There are God knows how many sheep in the fields, but I've no idea what kind they are.'

'Breeding for show is costly rather than profitable. I'll bet Abbott's one aim in life is to have a Stayforth ram declared best in show. Have a chat with him...'

'It's the manager's job to talk to the workers.'

'Then ask Ivor to do that.'

'If you mean Ballard, who used to be farm manager, he left months ago.'

'He was worth his weight in gold. What on earth caused him to leave?'

'I couldn't stand his insolence any longer. Kept arguing and wouldn't do as I said.'

'He worked the estate as if it were his own.'

'Which is precisely what I complained about.'

'Who's manager now?'

'I think he's called something like Goodall.'

'Then discuss things with him...'

'It's not my job to bother about the farm's running.'

'Perhaps not, but if you did...'

'All that can wait, since there's something that has to be dealt with right now. You do remember that the house you live in was Jerome's, not the trust's, so now it's mine?'

'Of course.'

'I'm going to have to ask you to pay rent.'

He stared at her in disbelief.

'I've made enquiries about present-day rates—'

He interrupted her. 'Jerome said we could live in Ca'n Dento rent free.'

'He was often far too generous. It's my experience that people don't appreciate what they don't pay for.'

'I can assure you, we've always appreciated his generosity.'

'The estate agent I spoke to – such an unintelligent man – told me the current rent for the house I described would be between five and seven hundred euros a month, depending on the state of the interior. Since Jerome provided the best equipment everywhere, the higher figure would obviously be more appropriate, but in the circumstances, I only intend to charge the lower one.'

Laura said, her words encased in ice: 'Are you not worried we won't fully appreciate your generosity?'

'There's something else. Dale's school fees are paid by the trust. That can't continue after the summer term and you will have to meet the fees from the autumn term onwards.'

'That's impossible.'

'It's necessary. I simply cannot afford to continue as things are.'

Laura, now speaking in as placatory a tone as she could summon, said: 'If we have to find the rent, there's absolutely no way in which we can meet the fees. Surely the trust could continue paying them for a while in the hopes things pick up for us?'

'To help you, I had a word with Sue over

the phone. She says that the local schools are surprisingly good and she'd recommend them to anyone.'

'Then why does she send her son to Eton?'

'In her position, obviously she has no option ... Dale would soon fit in.'

'When he's fifteen and working like hell for good exam results? When he speaks a little Spanish, but nowhere near enough to cope with a foreign curriculum? When much of the schooling, anyway, is now done in Mallorquin?'

'Children adapt very quickly.'

'Yet it seems Fergus was unable to adapt to conditions at Barnsford Close.'

'The staff were incompetently biased and refused to understand he has a very sensitive nature. I'm sorry, Laura, but we all have to make economies.'

'And some of us at other people's expense.' Laura stood. 'I think it'll be best if we leave now. Thank you for having us.'

As they walked across the lawn, Laura said, with angry fear: 'What are the school fees now?'

'Approaching twenty thousand a year,' Gerrard replied.

'Then we simply haven't a hope.'

'No.'

She came to a stop as they reached the

steps in the wall. 'Jerome promised the trust would see Dale through school and university.'

'I know.' He climbed down the steps and reached up to provide support as she followed.

'Then you've got to make the trustees honour his promise, whatever that woman says.' She stepped on to the ground.

'Jerome never put it in writing; even if he had, I don't know what force the promise would have.'

She swore, something she seldom did. She started to walk toward Ca'n Dento, taking short steps to avoid losing her balance on the rock- and stone-strewn ground. 'She wants five hundred euros a month for rent. How much is that in real money?'

'Call it three hundred and sixty pounds at the present rate of exchange.'

'Something over four thousand a year. If we have to pay her that, life is going to become really difficult.'

They reached the front door, made from planks of wood which had become warped by time and striated by weather. He unlocked it and stood to one side to let her enter.

She came to a stop in the middle of the sitting-room, under the overhead, locally made wrought-iron 'chandelier'. 'She can't possibly be as hard up as she's making out unless she's become impossibly extravagant.'

'Perhaps it will help if I have a word with her, explain just how financially strapped we are, and ask her to reconsider?'

'A waste of time.'

'Maybe not.'

'Charles, she's not acting like she is just because she wants more money – she's enjoying making you squirm.'

'That's rather dramatic.'

'Have you really never understood how bitterly she resents you?'

'Why should she? I've always been perfectly pleasant to her.'

'Which she interprets as condescension. It doesn't matter what your attitude really is, what counts for her is what she thinks it is. She's convinced you look down on her because of her background and it gives her enormous pleasure to get her own back.'

'I find it hard to accept that.'

'Because you're too good-natured.'

'You really do think she could be such a bitch?'

'Without even trying.'

Three

Gerrard stared at the sheet of paper in the typewriter. One day the words came in a rush, another, like the whining schoolboy, creeping unwillingly. But when one faced financial blackout, one's imagination became fixed on disaster and the words vanished.

Traditionally, younger brothers in families with landed estates joined the navy or the army or the Church, read for the Bar, or became sottish ne'er-do-wells. He had never wanted to kill anyone, had found it difficult to believe in a supreme being who allowed so much pain, had been reluctant to make a living out of other people's problems, and had no wish to follow in the footsteps of his great-great-uncle who had become a seven-bottle man before he died with a liver in such a state of decay that mention of it was still to be found in medical textbooks. He had decided he wanted to become an author – an ambition his family had thought so bizarre, they had persuaded him to join a firm of commodity brokers in which a relation was a Senior partner. It had taken little time to discover he did not wish to spend his working life buying, from people he never met, commodities he never saw and sold to whoever was at the other end of the telephone. He had quit the job, lived in one of the smaller estate houses and begun to write. Eventually, a script was accepted by a publisher who did not allow accountants to make all the editorial decisions. The first book had sold sufficiently well to encourage him to imagine his name on a best-seller list. He slowly learned that an optimistic author was one who lacked experience...

'Lunch,' Laura called out from downstairs.

The morning's work – one page which would have to be rewritten. He made his way down the concrete stairs to the sitting-room and went through to the kitchen.

She looked at him, then down at the saucepan in which she had cooked her version of Arróz brut. 'I've been thinking...'

'She thinks too much; such women are dangerous.'

'We can't just laugh everything away.'

'True.'

'I've been thinking what on earth we can do.'

'What else, but soldier on?'

'And if she continues to demand rent?'

'Remind her of the difficulty of getting blood out of a stone.'

'Knowing her, if we don't pay, she'll have us thrown out of here.'

'The Mallorquins are far too equitably-minded to allow her to do that.'

'I wish...'

'That I had a proper job?'

'No. Bloody no! You're doing what you want to do and I wouldn't change that for anything ... Get plates out, will you?'

He opened the door of one of the units and brought out two plates which he put on the polished granite work surface by the cooker.

'I'm going to ask her to change her mind,' she said suddenly.

'Yesterday, you vetoed the suggestion I should do so.'

She picked up a large kitchen spoon. 'If I do the asking, maybe she won't be so nasty-minded since I'm not of the family blood. I'll remind her how Jerome always tried to help you if he could. I have to do something, Charles. And asking her can't make things any worse.' She spooned the mixture of rice, pork, green pepper, tomato, and garlic onto his plate. He carried this over to the small eating area at the far end of the kitchen, sat, picked up the opened bottle of wine, half filled the two glasses.

She had served herself and was about to sit down when there was a knock on the front door.

'Who on earth is so out of tune with local custom as to call at this time of day?' He made to stand.

'I'll go as I'm already up.' She left the kitchen.

He drank. He wondered if reminding Heloise how well he and Jerome had always got on together would persuade her to become more generous. Might that not have the opposite effect? But as Laura had said, the situation could hardly become any worse.

Laura returned. 'Two people looking for Heloise, directed here by a local because of the same name.' She sat. 'The woman said she used to work at Stayforth, but I couldn't remember her. Her only introduction was that her name was Dora.'

'Almost certainly, Dora Coates. A large mole on her nose and a habit of hissing as she speaks?'

'A sorry description, but accurate.'

'Her name reminds me of one of my father's with-the-port reminiscences. He knew a family who employed a parlour maid called Dora, who was always complaining about bad digestion. One of the under-gardeners claimed he had the gift of healing and if he laid his hands on her, she would never suffer stomach pains again. She discovered what a liar he was when the pangs of pregnancy began.'

'Only a man could imagine a woman would be that stupid.'

'I remember feeling sorry for Dora Coates because she seemed so clumsy, but for no good reason, I never liked her.'

'You'd have liked her nephew even less, which is why I carefully didn't suggest that they came in and interrupted our meal in order to meet you.'

Moments later, he said: 'This dirty rice is tasty.'

'Perhaps it would be even tastier if you called it by some other name.'

'I'll try to remember. More wine?'

'Just for once, yes, please.'

He replenished both their glasses.

'Dora is in for an unpleasant shock if she expects Heloise to welcome her, as a past employee,' she said.

'People on holiday tend to become

irrational … Is there any more Arróz brut left?'

'You said you were going to diet.'

'It was you who said I was.'

'You are putting on weight.'

'One of the benefits of middle age is a rounded personality.'

'I suppose if you have what's left, the scales won't break. Pass your plate.'

'I'll get it.' He stood. 'Halve what's left?'

'Thanks, but I've never learned the art of persuading a mirror to lie.'

He crossed to the cooker, spooned what remained in the saucepan onto his plate.

Four

As Dolores went through the bead curtain into the kitchen on Tuesday evening, Jaime reached out to the bottle of wine; when she unexpectedly reappeared, he tried to make out he was picking up the salt cellar.

She stared at him for a moment, her dark brown eyes filled with sharp suspicion, then said: 'I have made some Capxetas de merengue.'

'An unexpected pleasure!' Alvarez remarked enthusiastically.

'You think I am incapable of serving such a dish or that I am too lazy to do so?'

'It was just a way of saying how much I'm looking forward to enjoying your wonderful cooking.'

'You have a strange way of expressing yourself ... Put out some plates on the table.' She returned to the kitchen, leaving the trails of the bead curtain clashing into each other with diminishing force.

As Jaime refilled his glass with wine,

43

Alvarez said: 'What's got her into a mood?'

'How would I know?' Jaime drank.

'You're her husband.'

'What husband ever knows why his wife's bitching?'

'Have you been rowing with her?'

'You think I'm a fool?'

Alvarez thought him weak, not a fool. It was a husband's duty to make certain his wife showed a proper respect for him, yet by admitting he would never willingly argue with her, he was failing in his duty. 'Something's upset her.'

'Not necessarily. Women often get like that for no reason.'

Dolores returned, in her hand a large plate on which were meringues of ground almond, lemon, and a touch of cinnamon. She put the plate down on the table, but did not sit. 'I've every reason to be surprised, but of course am not.'

They nervously tried to work out what was now annoying her, but failed.

'You forgot I asked you to put out plates?'

'No,' Jaime answered hurriedly.

'Then why are they not on the table?'

'I was just going to get them.'

'After you had refilled your glass and drunk until your mind rose higher than the clouds? Aiyee! If men did all they said they

44

were going to, women would no longer have to spend their lives slaving.' She put the meringues on the table, went around Jaime's chair, opened one of the doors of the carved Mallorquin sideboard and brought out three small plates which she handed to Alvarez. 'I hope you will not find it too onerous to pass these around?'

Having done as asked, Alvarez helped himself to a meringue. It was delicious, as he had expected. Dolores was a wonderful cook; to such an extent that one tried to make allowances for her many faults.

There was a shout from upstairs. Dolores, her expression shocked, hastily came to her feet. 'Sweet Mary, what's happened?'

'Isabel's having a nightmare,' Jaime answered.

'You calmly sit there when she has perhaps fallen out of bed, broken her shoulder, and is lying in agony?' She pushed back her chair, rushed across the room and up the stairs.

'One of the kids has a dream and shouts,' Jaime said sourly, 'and she imagines the very worst. Yet I tell her I've a vicious pain in my belly and she merely says that's because I've drunk too much.' He leaned across and opened a door of the sideboard, brought out a bottle of brandy, poured himself a drink, passed the bottle to Alvarez. 'The husband always gets the rough edge, doesn't matter what he says or does.'

'A small price to pay if it keeps the wife happy.'

'What about the husband's happiness?'

'That's the price of marriage.'

Dolores came downstairs.

'Well?' Jaime demanded loudly as she stepped off the last stair on to the floor.

She approached her chair.

'Come on, then, has she fallen out of bed and broken her shoulder?' he demanded aggressively, enjoying the rare chance of proving his wife wrong.

'You have been consoling yourself in case she had?' She studied the bottle of brandy on the table.

'It was just a dream, wasn't it?'

'Whilst I was upstairs, I had a dream. Shall I tell you what it was?'

The question unsettled him.

'I dreamt you realised I was very tired; that wishing to help me, you had cleared the table so that when I came downstairs, I had nothing to do but sit and rest whilst you made the coffee. Of course, dreams are always absurd.'

'I was just about to clear.'

Did he ever think before he spoke? Alvarez

wondered.

'Another just about? How busy your future must always appear to you, especially when you have drunk enough to imagine yourself a thoughtful husband.'

'I've hardly drunk anything this evening.'

'The surprise is that you can still speak absurdities.' She began to clear the table by picking up the bottle of brandy and putting it in the sideboard.

Soon after she had returned from the kitchen and sat, watching the television with the other two, the phone rang. After a while, she said: 'You are both suddenly very hard of hearing?'

'This late, it has to be for you,' Jaime said.

'Naturally, since that provides an excuse for not disturbing yourself.' She stood. 'I have often wondered why the good Lord provided men with legs since they so seldom use them.' She went through to the next room, soon returned. 'It is someone from the Policia Local in the port.'

'They want me?' Alvarez asked. 'What's the matter?'

'Perhaps you wish me to return and ask if there is sufficient reason for you to bother yourself to speak to them?'

He went through to the front room, used only on formal occasions and kept in apple-pie order. He picked up the receiver. 'Alvarez.'

'We have a problem. An Englishman says his aunt is missing; she went for a swim roughly half an hour ago and seems to have disappeared.'

'Are you serious? Half an hour ago it was already dark.'

'So?'

'You're saying there's someone goes swimming in the dark?'

'She also is English.'

The English, ever perverse, had developed to perfection the art of upsetting other people's lives. 'It's likely she's still swimming.'

'Her nephew says she's a very poor swimmer and would never go out of her depth; he's searched close to the shore, but can't find her.'

'If she can't swim, why the hell did she go into the sea when it's dark and there'll be no one around to see if she gets into trouble?'

'She'd been drinking heavily.'

'Considering her nationality, that goes without saying. If she's drowned, why bother me? It's not my problem.'

'One of us went with the nephew to see if they could find her. A woman came up and when she heard what they were doing, told them she'd heard another woman crying out in English and saying something like, "What are you doing? Don't. Please don't." '

'That's all?'

'Yes.'

'What's the missing woman's name and where's she staying?'

'Dora Coates, at the Hotel Monterray.'

'You'd better get a boat out and see if there's any sign of her in the bay.'

'It's up to you to search.'

'Not when there's nothing to suggest any criminal activity.'

'You're never going to die from overwork.'

He replaced the receiver. The members of the Policia Local were forever trying to get out of doing their job.

Alvarez made his way downstairs to the kitchen. Dolores, stirring the contents of a saucepan on the stove, looked up. 'I called you long ago. Another five minutes and you'd have had to get your own breakfast since I've a mountain of work to do.'

He sat at the table. Clearly, her perverse mood of the previous evening had not improved.

'Shouldn't you be at work by now?' she asked.

'When there's not much doing, it's left to

a person's judgement as to when he starts.'

'Whoever decided it should be left to you was no judge of character.'

'That's not fair.'

'When a man starts bleating something is unfair, one can be certain his conscience has finally been touched ... You can have yesterday's bread or you'll have to go out and buy a barra.' She ceased stirring, scraped the spoon clean on the edge of the saucepan, turned off the gas. 'Well, which is it to be?'

Why hadn't she made certain he had fresh bread for his breakfast? 'Is something wrong?'

'Why do you ask?'

'You seem so ... I wondered if maybe there was some sort of trouble?'

'With two men and two children to look after, there is always trouble.'

'But nothing serious, I hope?'

'As my mother so wisely observed, "For a man, nothing is serious unless he is incommoded." '

'She doesn't seem to have had a very good opinion of men.'

'How could she, having many brothers and a husband for fifty-one years? ... You may have time to waste talking, I do not. Will you buy yourself a fresh barra or eat the one from yesterday?'

'You could put that in the oven to crisp it up, couldn't you?'

'You are incapable of doing even that? Adam must have lost more than his rib to have left all men so hopeless.'

'And what happened after his rib was taken?' he asked, resentful of the suggestion that he was motivated by laziness. 'Eve persuaded him to eat the forbidden fruit.'

'No doubt only after she had prepared it for him. I suppose you want some hot chocolate?'

'Would you be very kind and make me some?'

'As if I could imagine you would do it for yourself!' She moved the saucepan. 'Have you ever wondered what is a woman's greatest burden? Of course you haven't, so I will tell you. It is sympathy for the weakness of a man, because this causes her blindly to accept that it is her duty to obey his wishes, that it is his right to be waited on hand and foot, that he is entitled to indulge his every desire and ignore all hers. And how does he express his thanks? By fresh demands. No doubt, you are about to ask me again to warm the bread as well as make the chocolate?'

'I'll do that,' he said hastily.

'And reduce the barra to a cinder? As my

51

mother so often cautioned me, "There is only one thing at which a man excels and that is incompetence." ' She went over to the bread bin and brought out a barra, crossed to the sink and used her fingers to brush a dusting of water over it, put it in the oven and lit the gas. She collected up the ingredients for hot chocolate and carried them back to the stove. When she next spoke, her manner had softened. 'I met Benito yesterday in the supermarket.'

'Benito?'

'Ortega. He is back from Argentina.'

'Didn't expect to hear from him again.'

'Times have changed both there and here. And as he said to me, the older one becomes, the more one misses one's country of birth. He is looking to own a grand property since now he is a man of great presence.'

'Only in his own mind.'

She poured hot chocolate into a mug, put that on the table. 'If he is not very wealthy, how can Luisa wear so many fine jewels?'

'They'll all be false.'

'You think I can't tell the difference?'

He was certain she couldn't, but was not prepared to say so. 'If genuine, they're wasted on Luisa.'

'Why do you say that?'

'As I remember her, even air-brushing wouldn't help.'

'How like a man! Considers only what he sees and ignores what lies hidden. A woman may be a saint, but unless a man thinks her beautiful, he scorns her.'

'Luisa's never been a saint.'

'Now what are you suggesting?'

'There was at least one man who sought and found what lay hidden.'

'Nonsense!'

'It was common knowledge.'

'As is all cruel slander, made all the crueller by mindless repetition.' She turned off the gas in the oven, brought out the barra, put it on the bread board and this on the table. 'What else do you want?'

'Is there any honey?'

She put a pot down by the bread. 'Who was named?'

He cut a length of barra, sliced it in half. 'You wouldn't want me to add to the cruel repetition, would you?'

'Was it Mauricio Campos?'

'You think he had the cojones?'

'Then who?'

'Luis Guillen.'

'Ridiculous! Nothing could be more absurd.'

'Why?'

'If you cannot answer, you must remain ignorant.'

'Have you never asked yourself why he enjoyed such a succession of ladies?'

'I do not insult myself with such questions.'

'He always told them they were safe with him because his interests were different. Those who believed him soon found out their mistake.'

'To lie about such things! Have men no shame?'

He ate.

After a while, she sat. 'Benito is thinking he will buy Son Estar.'

'Him in a possessío. That would be like a tramp sitting on a golden throne.'

'Things have changed.'

'Not that much. In any case, he's too old to own an estate that's so run down it'll need a mountain of work to get it back in order.'

'He will hope someone will join the family who can help him. He has but one child, Eva. Daughters marry.'

'If she has her mother's looks and character, only a man who's half-blind as well as half-witted will marry her.'

She pushed back her chair and stood. 'There is more wisdom to be found in a donkey's bray than a man's words.' She swept out of the kitchen.

He drank some chocolate, tore off a piece of barra, buttered it, added honey, ate. Woman had been defined as a riddle wrapped in a mystery inside an enigma. How could there be any logical explanation for Dolores's sudden anger ... A thought abruptly provided one. Like all women, she believed a man needed to be instructed and corrected and this was best done by a wife. If Benito truly was wealthy enough to buy Son Estar, then Eva's husband would eventually share her inheritance of the manor house, several fincas, two hundred hectares of good land, orange and olive groves, fields of almond trees, three deep wells, and half a mountain. Even in his wildest dreams, he never imagined himself in possession of such an estate, yet perhaps now ... Dreams addled the brain. Had life not taught him that even as one enjoys the sunshine, one should be preparing for either a drought or a downpour? Under Mallorquin law, Eva would own the property in her own name so would she ever be prepared to accept her husband's authority if there were a disagreement between them?

Five

Alvarez drove over the torrente – now a dried-up, boulder-strewn river bed, occasionally in the winter a raging, dangerous flood – and along the Palma–Port Llueso road. Five minutes later, he parked under the shade of a tree, then walked to the guardia post, to arrive sweating and slightly breathless. He nodded at the duty cabo, who barely acknowledged the greeting – the young were becoming ever less mannered – and climbed the stairs to his room, which left him sweating more freely and definitely breathless. He slumped down in the chair behind the desk and stared blankly at the closed widow and shutters which for the moment he lacked the energy to open. Perhaps his doctor had reason – he was out of condition and did need to lose weight, give up smoking, and drink far less. Why was medicine dedicated to denying pleasure?

There were several unopened letters on the desk, left there earlier by the duty cabo.

If they remained unopened, he wouldn't know if one of them called upon him to do something. It was only the twenty-first of May, yet already the days were so soporifically hot...

He was awakened by the phone. As he waited in the hope the caller would impatiently disconnect, he looked at his watch and was surprised to note it was time for his merienda. Since the ringing continued, he reached out and picked up the receiver.

'Inspector Alvarez?'

'Speaking.'

'Policia Local, Port Playa Neuva. The body of Señorita Coates had just been recovered.'

'Who?'

The name was repeated.

'Recovered from where?'

'It was not you who Pedro, in Port Llueso, rang last night?'

'It was me, yes.'

'Then surely he told you Señorita Coates was missing after going swimming in Llueso Bay?'

'Of course ... My problem is, my work is endless and I'm sometimes at my desk eighteen hours in the day so that my mind becomes over-burdened and I can't remember things immediately. So how was the

Señorita found?'

'A tourist from Hotel Playa Tanit went snorkelling and found a body amongst the seaweed, some four hundred metres out from the shore. He told the hotel receptionist who phoned us and one of our chaps put on the gear, dived down and pulled her ashore. Señor Short, her nephew, was asked to make an identification, which he has.'

'Then everything's sorted and there's no call for me to be further concerned in the matter.'

'You'd better have a word with the doctor who examined the body before you decide that.'

'Why?'

'He says there may be an ambiguity about her death.'

'She didn't drown?'

'That's not the problem.'

'Then what is?'

'Can't rightly tell, but the doctor said the Cuerpo had to be called in.'

'Then I suppose I'll have to find out what's bothering him. I'll be over as soon as I can make it.'

'He says he's very busy and you must get there right away.'

And miss his merienda at Club Llueso?

* * *

58

'I've been waiting over half an hour,' Dr Garzon said with angry impatience. 'Were you not told to get here right away?'

'I'm sorry about that,' Alvarez answered, 'but something very pressing held me back in Llueso.'

'And left me standing around.' Garzon had a habit of thrusting his pointed chin forward, adding an air of further belligerence. 'Don't just stand there – follow me.'

The morgue at the back of the undertaker's office had been modernised and now visually bore a resemblance to an operating theatre – walls and floor were tiled, there were two adjustable examination tables, sinks, work surfaces, and cupboards were of stainless steel, and there was an overhead, trackable light pod. A body, covered with a green sheet, was on the nearer table. The doctor pulled the sheet back.

The sight of death always affected Alvarez badly since familiarity never reduced its cruel reminder that he was mortal and one day it would find him.

'The p.m. will confirm my judgement that the cause of death was drowning.'

Garzon, Alvarez thought, as he tried to look anywhere but at the dead woman and in consequence found himself repeatedly staring at her, never suffered the thought he could be wrong.

'Taking into account the temperature of the water and the body, the degree of rigor remaining, the wrinkling of the skin on hands and feet, I place death as having occurred between nine and midnight on Tuesday.'

'There's reason to think she didn't die accidentally?'

'The possibility has to be considered.'

'Why's that?'

'What do you know about drowning?'

'Nothing, thankfully.'

Garzon joined his hands together behind his back, held up his head, and spoke as if giving a lecture to fractious students. 'Immediately preceding death, even if a suicidal act, the victim will struggle. On my initial examination of the victim, I found that under the fingernails of both hands were many grains of sand, sufficiently embedded to show the hands had been dug into sand with considerable force. You can understand the significance of this?'

'If in her struggles she dug her hands into sand, she must have been in shallow water. So why didn't she save herself merely by standing up? The report I've received states she had been drinking heavily before she went swimming. Perhaps she was too drunk to try to save herself. There are cases where drunks have drowned in a puddle.'

'Quite,' said Garzon, showing his surprise that Alvarez should appreciate the possible significance of the facts. 'I examined the body very closely, but the only visible sign of trauma was a small incision on the back of the head, probably, though not certainly, incurred before death.'

'How important is that?'

'Difficult to be precise.'

'Suppose her head was being forced under water until she drowned, could the wound have been inflicted during this time?'

'It's possible to envisage a fingernail bearing down on the scalp and her struggles causing the nail to pierce the skin.'

'You can't be more positive?'

'I cannot.'

'So you can't decide whether or not this was murder?'

'My task is to give you the medical facts. I have done so.'

'If she was so drunk she'd lost the natural instinct of self-preservation, would she have been able to walk from the hotel to the sea?'

'I cannot answer that.'

'I'll need to know her alcohol level.'

'I have naturally taken the necessary samples for analysis,' Garzon said pompously.

As Alvarez drove along the road which ringed the bay, his thoughts were gloomy. Dr Garzon had enough self-confidence for two, yet had been unable to determine whether the case was one of accidental death or murder. As a consequence, Superior Chief Salas would have to be informed of the problem and this meant endless trouble and a workload increased to unbearable limits. Except it would have to be borne.

One did not rush towards trouble. He stopped the car and parked just off the road on the sand, a few metres short of the nearest heap of seaweed, thrown up during the winter, which in good time would be removed and stored in clamps until fit to use as fertiliser. As he stared out at the mountain-ringed bay – its beauty unequalled anywhere in the world – his depression began to lift. As the doctor had indicated, the incision on the scalp might well have been caused in any one of the many minor accidental injuries anyone suffered throughout life; Dora Coates might well have drunk to the point where she was able to stagger to the water but was incapable of saving herself from drowning; the cries which had been heard were likely to have been uttered by a tourist who discovered it wasn't just her beauty which excited her companion. The case might well only call for a little extra work on his part.

He drove back to Llueso by the slower route and as he passed the small fields, bounded by stone walls, he studied with a critical eye the flocks of sheep and goats, the occasional crop of rye grass, sunflowers, wheat, or barley, the vineyard of dessert grapes, and he sadly noted how much land was left untended because few young were willing to work it when money was so much more easily earned in the tourist trade ... What if that one trade on which the island's prosperity now depended were suddenly to vanish? There were few industries which were not tourist-orientated and there would be next to nothing to export in order to earn the money which would be needed for imports. Would the islanders be forced back to an even harsher life than their forefathers had suffered because now there were so few who had the skills and knowledge to produce the food desperately needed?

Back in his office, he sat and stared at the telephone on his desk. Perhaps Salas was away at one of the many conferences he attended; he might not be well; he might ... Vain hopes. To wish for something to happen was to ensure it did not; to wish for something not to happen was to ensure it did. He dialled.

'Yes?' said the secretary who always sounded as if she had a plum in her mouth.

'I'd like a word with the superior chief.'

'You have a name?'

'Inspector Alvarez.'

'Wait.'

It was difficult to decide who was the more rudely curt, she or her employer.

'What do you want?' was Salas's greeting.

'Señor, yesterday evening when we were having supper ... or was it just after we'd finished eating?'

'I am uninterested in the details of your domestic life.'

'I'm just trying to sort out things in my own mind.'

'One can appreciate the difficulty of that.'

'It was probably some time after eleven o'clock when there was a phone call from the Policia Local in...'

'An official call?'

'Yes, Señor.'

'Then refer to your communications log so that you can give me an exact time.'

'But I was at home.'

'So you have already said.'

'I don't have the communications log

at home.'

'You did not make a note yesterday evening of the time and then transfer that to your log this morning when you arrived at the office? It seems not ... I suppose you will not be aware that after listening to you for several minutes, I still have not the slightest idea what you are trying to tell me.'

'Señor, I was about to explain when you objected to what I was saying.'

'With good reason. But now, perhaps you can bring yourself to explain what was the import of the phone call from the Policia Local?'

'An English woman who was staying at Hotel Monterray in Port Llueso, Dora Coates, went swimming on Tuesday night after dark. When she didn't return, her nephew became worried and searched for her, couldn't find her, and reported her absence. It was later ascertained that a woman on the beach reported hearing a cry in English which was something like, "What are you doing? Don't. Please don't," but there was no certainty the call had come from the sea, not the beach; and if from the beach, what more likely than that it had been made by another woman...'

'Why should you believe that?'

'The words strongly suggested a woman

65

who had been encouraging a man by in-
action and then...'

'How does one encourage inactively?'

'By doing nothing.'

'If one is doing nothing, one is not encouraging.'

'Yes, if one should be discouraging.'

'Words can enable a listener to understand
what would otherwise be inexplicable.
Unfortunately, they also have the ability
to make what should be simple, totally
opaque. Will you explain, in the simplest
terms of which you are capable, just what in
the devil you are talking about?'

'When a young man and woman are alone
together on a warm night, in the dark, the
man is very likely to become amorous. If she
doesn't stop him early on, he thinks he'll be
allowed to go all the way; but when she
discovers that's what he reckons, she may
panic and beg him to stop in words such as
were heard.'

There was a pause before Salas said: 'Experience should have reminded me of your
perverse interest in a subject ignored by
those of even moderate refinement.'

'My interest isn't any greater than anyone
else's.'

'That you can make so absurd a claim is
proof you are in need of psychiatric help.'

Salas cut the connection.

Alvarez replaced the receiver, leaned over and opened the bottom right-hand drawer of the desk, and brought out a bottle of Soberano and a glass; he poured himself a large drink.

The phone rang. He put the glass down, lifted the receiver. 'Inspector Alvarez, Cuerpo...'

'Unfortunately, you have no need to introduce yourself,' Salas said bitterly. 'There is not another officer in the Cuerpo who phones his superior to make a report and spends minutes recounting his domestic arrangements before he displays the perversity of his interests and then rings off without another word.'

'Señor, it was not I who rang off...'

'Make your report!'

Minutes later, Alvarez replaced the receiver, picked up the glass, and drank. He looked at his watch and decided he could soon return home for lunch since Salas was hardly likely to ring a third time. He wondered what Dolores would have cooked. Espinagada? A pastry filled with fresh eel, garlic, onions, hot pepper, and he knew not what else. Of course, this was the traditional dish for the feast of Saint Anthony, when it was eaten in the warmth of bonfires in the streets whilst insolent songs, accompanied by ximbombas, were sung, but that was no reason for not serving it at other times and Dolores knew how much he liked it.

Six

In the past forty years, Port Llueso had in many ways changed more than in the previous four hundred. Once a small fishing village, now it was a tourist resort with a large marina, and although there was a ban on high apartment blocks or hotels so that it was no concrete jungle, anyone who could remember its past sleepy charm was saddened by its present ambience.

Alvarez left the police station and climbed into his car. Hotel Monterray was not far away, but it was only common sense not to exert oneself unnecessarily when the temperature was high. He drove up to the small roundabout by the eastern harbour mole, past a No Entry sign, and along the pedestrianised front road, to the obvious annoyance of several foreigners. He parked and once out of the car, stared at the beach. Hotel and restaurant owners were complaining that the number of tourists was down and they were spending little, but to judge from all those sunbathing, swimming, or sitting at the outside café tables, the complaints had more to do with tax returns than facts.

Hotel Monterray, one of the oldest hotels in the port, had been greatly enlarged twenty years before, yet much of its previous character had been maintained; package-holiday brochures referred to it as a quiet family hotel and for once were not guilty of lying. The lobby was well proportioned, the few pieces of furniture of good quality; the reception counter was made from a rich, dark wood and kept well polished, while the clerk, or clerks (two were usually on duty when a busload of tourists was expected), wore ties, however hot the day, and were always respectfully polite no matter what the provocation to which they were sub-jected.

Alvarez spoke to the clerk behind the reception desk. 'Evening, Diego.'

'Not seen you for some time. Been on holiday?'

'Working.'

'There's a difference? ... Something you want?'

'A word with Señor Short.'

'There's a reason?'

'What's it to you?'

'It's just the Cuerpo doesn't usually bother with accidental deaths.'

'Foreigners confuse everything.'

'So true. Who else goes swimming in the dark and after drinking a skinful?'

'How tight did she appear to be?'

'You'll have to ask Gaspar that – he's on night shift. From what he told me, her nephew was trying hard to dissuade her from swimming, but she wasn't listening.'

'Then I'll need a word with Gaspar as well. When does he come on duty?'

'Should be six, always it's some time past. I'll win the lottery before he relieves me on time.'

Alvarez looked up at the electric clock on the wall behind the reception desk. 'He'll be here before long, then, but I've time for a word with Señor Short, if he's around?'

Diego studied the key board. 'Seems he's up in his room. Could be grieving, but that seems unlikely.'

'Hardly a Christian remark.'

'She was pure vinegar. Never a smile and if she had to speak to one of us, it was giving orders rather than a friendly request. Of course, it was likely the booze speaking.'

'Then you can confirm she was a heavy drinker much of the time?'

'Elena – serves at the tables when it's not

a buffet meal – says it was always her, not him, who ordered another bottle of wine and like as not, finished most of it, talking louder and louder. Didn't make her popular with the other guests; you'd see 'em move away smartly if she came in sight ... Shouldn't be talking like this, not now she's dead.'

'I've never known death turn black into white ... Just check he is in his room, will you; might save me a wasted journey.'

Diego spoke briefly in English over the internal telephone, put the palm of his hand over the mouthpiece. 'Wants to know if you'll go up or he's to come downstairs?'

'Down here will be best to begin with. Is there somewhere we can be on our own?'

'Use the office. There's no one working in there at the moment.'

After passing the message to Short and replacing the receiver, Diego lifted the flap at the end of the counter to allow Alvarez to pass through and into the office, a small room made even less commodious by two desks, filing cabinets, and a large bookcase.

'What would you say if management offered you a complimentary drink?' Diego asked.

'That I was taught it was bad manners to refuse a gift.'

Diego returned outside, closing the door behind himself. Alvarez sat. There was the sound of conversation, then the door was opened. 'Señor Short,' Diego said.

'My name is Inspector Alvarez, of the Cuerpo General de Policia,' he said, as he stood and held out his hand. 'I'm very sorry to trouble you at so sad a time, but I fear it is necessary.'

They both sat. Years ago, Alvarez thought, he would have judged Short a potential trouble-maker, always fighting authority simply because it was authority – long hair, tied in a pony-tail, one earring, designer stubble, rough clothing, and an aggressive expression would have branded him. But in the modern world, the only challenge of so many whose appearance matched his was against good taste. 'What I should like you to do, Señor, is to tell me what happened yesterday evening.'

Short hesitated, then said: 'Is something wrong?'

'When there is a fatal accident, there has to be a brief investigation to determine all the details – one of the reasons for which is that the information may lead to better safety measures and prevent a repetition.'

'Yeah, I can see that. It's just I thought that with you being a detective, there must be a problem.'

'Have you any reason to think there might be one?'

'No way.'

There was a knock on the door, which was opened, and a waiter, carrying a tray, entered. 'Who's the coñac for?'

'Me,' Alvarez answered.

The waiter handed him the smaller glass, the larger one to Short.

The brandy proved to be of a good quality, showing that despite a certain facetiousness, Diego had a proper respect for the Cuerpo. 'After you have told me what you can, Señor, I will need to search the Señorita's room, then I should not need to trouble you again.'

'Search her room?'

'It is always necessary when a foreigner dies for the possessions to be assembled and held until instructions are given as to what to do with them.'

'I suppose.'

'You and your aunt arrived here when?'

'Thursday.'

'You were very friendly with her, coming away on holiday together?'

'It's like this. She and my dad didn't get on and I never saw much of her until he died and she came to the funeral. I made a bit of a point of looking after her – how one does – and that must have gone down well because afterwards she was often in touch. But to tell the truth, it was still a surprise when she said she was having a holiday and she'd like me to come along for someone to talk to. She knew I'd been made redundant months before and so I wondered if she was just being kind rather than needing company. Or maybe trying to kind of make up for some of the things Dad told me she'd said to him.'

'Was she a wealthy lady?'

'She had enough, but she wasn't rolling in it.'

'Why did she come to Port Llueso for a holiday?'

'I wouldn't know.'

'Perhaps she had been here before or had read about it in the paper?'

'Could be.'

'But she never said so?'

'That's right, she didn't.'

'She was a keen swimmer?'

'Liked it, all right, but wasn't much of a one; more a paddler.'

'Yet she went swimming after dark when it had to be unlikely someone would notice if she got into trouble?'

'I tried to stop her. Fact is, we had a bit of

a row about it, but she wouldn't listen because...'

'Yes?'

'Don't like saying this. She used to drink and by the time she said she wanted to swim, she wasn't thinking straight.'

'Which you think is why she refused to listen to you?'

'Yeah.'

'Had she always been a heavy drinker?'

'It was about the only thing my dad never accused her of, so maybe she wasn't when she was younger. But after his funeral the people came back for a drink and a bite and she had rather more than she could handle. I can remember thinking, if Dad was looking down at what was going on, he'd have told anyone who'd listen that he wasn't surprised.'

'Your aunt drank quite heavily and insisted on going swimming, despite the fact it was night-time and you advised her not to?'

'That's how it went.'

'You didn't go with her to make certain she was all right?'

'No ... And you think I don't keep saying to myself I ought to have done because then she'd have been OK? Only I stayed in the hotel and had a drink at the bar with blokes

I'd met because she became nasty when I kept on trying to persuade her not to go and I got to think that if that's how she wanted things, that's how she could have 'em. Couldn't have been more bloody stupid, could I? If I'd ignored the things she was saying, she'd be alive now. And I knew it wasn't her talking, it was the booze.'

'You had a drink at the bar. Was it just one?'

'Two, three maybe. Then I started to worry because I hadn't seen her come back; had a word with the receptionist and he hadn't see her either, so I went out to the beach. Found her towel, but there wasn't no sign of her.'

'What did you do next?'

'Went along the beach both ways, shouting, walked into the water, ran back to the hotel and said she must be in trouble and I needed a torch, went on searching. In the end I came back and said they must call the police.'

'You were convinced she had drowned?'

'What else could I think?'

'Thank you for telling me all this, Señor. Now, if you will accompany me to her room?'

They left the office and after Diego had given Alvarez the key, took the lift up to the first floor – climbing stairs was acknowledged to be a stressful exercise.

No. 15 was a large room with two single beds and an outside balcony, furnished in good hotel style. On one of the two chairs were clothes, neatly folded – clearly those she had been wearing before she went swimming. There were three frocks and two pairs of shoes in the cupboard, blouses, tights, and underclothes in the two top drawers of the chest-of-drawers; in the bottom drawer was a very good-quality handbag. He opened it, brought out a bundle of hundred-euro notes and a few travellers' cheques. He counted the amounts. 'There are a hundred and fifty euros in cheques and two thousand, two hundred and fifty euros in notes.'

'Yeah?'

'That's a large amount in cash.'

'More than I've seen a for a long time, that's for sure.'

'From a safety point, when travelling it's unusual to carry so much in cash and so little in cheques. Do you know why she chose to have so much in cash?'

'No idea. If she'd asked, I'd have said it was barmy because one never knows if some little toe-rag will nick it.'

'How old was she?'

'Dad always said she was two years

younger than him which would make her sixty-eight.'

'Did she still work?'

'Stopped some time back.'

'What work did she do?'

'She was in domestic service. Started off as a lady's maid and retired as a house-keeper. Leastwise, that's what she'd always tell you; Dad said she was just a general help but liked the grander name.'

Alvarez brought the rest of the contents out of the handbag – passport, air ticket, diary, lace-edged handkerchief, nail file, compact, folded-up piece of paper, and a very elegant heart-shaped gold locket with a small diamond under the inverted peak. He unfolded the square of paper. 'Do you know Lady Gerrard?'

'Who?'

He repeated the name.

'Never heard of her.'

'Then you can't tell me why your aunt wrote down the name or even if the person lives here or in England?'

'That's right, I can't.'

'I'll replace everything in the handbag and then take it downstairs to be held in the hotel safe until I learn what to do with the contents.'

'Hang on. I ... It's like I don't have any

money.'

'You were relying on your aunt to provide what you needed?'

'Yes,' he mumbled. Then more firmly: 'Like I said, I've been having to live on the dole.'

'In the circumstances, since your aunt would have provided you with money, while it may not be legally correct to do so, I will give you two hundred euros from your aunt's money.'

'Thank God for that! I was thinking I'd be stuck here without a quid to my name.'

'I will need your receipt.'

'Sure.'

Alvarez put two notes to one side, replaced everything else back in the handbag. 'We'll return below now.'

Downstairs, Diego gave Alvarez two sheets of headed notepaper. On the first, Alvarez detailed the contents of the handbag, specifying the amount in cash and cheques; on the second, he wrote 'Received from the cash found in Señorita Dora Coates's handbag, the sum of two hundred euros for personal use.' He and Short signed the first, Short the second. Diego was given the handbag to be put into the hotel's safe.

'Thank you, Señor,' Alvarez said to Short.

'That's all?'

'I may have to speak to you again, but for the moment I do not need to trouble you any more.'

Short said goodbye, crossed the foyer to leave the hotel.

'So is there now a problem?' Diego asked.

'Why should there be?'

'How would I know?'

'You wouldn't, but like all hotel staff, you have an insatiable interest in other people's affairs ... There's something you can tell me.'

'With pleasure. You're goddamn rude.'

'Do you know a Lady Gerrard?'

'Me, a desk clerk, know an English aristocrat who bathes in asses' milk?'

'There is always the chance you've helped to provide the milk. You've not come across the name?'

'Why do you ask?'

'Idle curiosity.'

'As if you could ever suffer energetic curiosity! No, I don't think I've ever heard it. Except it seems ... Of course! Soon after they'd arrived, Señorita Coates came up and said Lady Gerrard lived locally, could I tell her where?'

'Was Señor Short with her at the time?'

'I think so.' After further thought, he said: 'Yes, he definitely was. I remember him saying they ought to phone her first.'

'Were you able to tell her where Lady Gerrard lived?'

'I said that if she was on the phone, the address would be in the telephone book.'

'So now be kind enough to find out if it is.'

Diego reached under the counter and produced a directory, turned to the section covering Llueso. 'Here we are. Ca'n Jerome. It's sin numero, so it's in the country.'

Alvarez thanked the other, looked up at the clock. 'Your relief ought to be here very soon.'

'But won't be.'

Escobar arrived eleven minutes late and as he moved behind the counter, a stout woman, sufficiently ill-advised to wear shorts, her heavy face expressing angry determination, approached; Diego hastily left.

'Can I help, Señora?' Escobar asked in English as she came to a stop.

'I don't think you lot could help a blind beggar,' was her strident answer.

'What is the trouble, Señora?'

'I'll tell you. Me and Dad paid good money for this holiday and the brochure said as you was known for the quality of the grub. So what did you dish up today? Beans what didn't have no tomato sauce and there was lumps of red, messy stuff what looked real nasty.'

'I think that was chorizo. I can assure you it is delicious...'

'Maybe the likes of you enjoy it, but that's because you don't know no better. But I'm not touching it. So you tell the cook that if he doesn't dish up some decent grub the next meal, I'm making the travel rep move us somewhere else. If there is anywhere what knows what good grub is.' She stalked off.

'What has so upset her?' Alvarez asked.

'The new manager is full of strange ideas and said people coming on holiday to Spain should enjoy Spanish food, so once a week there's a classic dish. At lunch it was Alubias con chorizo. The chef's a genius at making it.'

As great a genius as Dolores? Alvarez wondered. She could take butter beans, onions, garlic, olive oil, sweet paprika, parsley, and chorizo, and produce a dish that would make a man's mouth water merely to think about it. 'I need to ask you one or two questions about Señorita Coates. Perhaps we could sit down somewhere?'

'Not with me having to be at the desk to explain to the guests they aren't being poisoned.'

Then he'd have to continue to stand. 'How did she and the nephew get on together?'

'Bit difficult to answer. I mean, the two of them would argue, but who doesn't?'

'Did they argue often?'

'She did, and most times it was him trying to calm her down. And if she'd been drinking, he didn't get very far.'

'You suggested earlier, she liked the bottle.'

'You don't see many women as attached to it as she was.'

'Would you say she was drunk when she went for a swim last night?'

'Had to be, wanting to go in the dark. He tried to stop her; said she couldn't swim well and shouldn't be out on her own, but she wouldn't listen.'

'It's slightly odd he didn't go with her if he was so concerned.'

'After all she'd said to him? He let her get on with it and went into the bar, same as anyone else would have done. After a while he came out and asked if she'd returned and when I told him she hadn't, said he must see she was all right. The next thing, he's dripping wet, yelling for a torch and to call the police.'

'How long was there between her leaving here and his going out to try to find her?'

'Can't rightly say. There was paperwork to do and more of the guests were asking fool questions than usual ... If you want a guess, a quarter of an hour, twenty minutes.'

'And how long between his going out and returning to raise the alarm?'

'Could have been the same or a bit more.'

'So he must have been searching quite hard?'

'From the look of him, he'd almost been swimming ... Something funny been going on?'

'What makes you think that?'

'You asking questions.'

'All I'm doing is tying to tidy up everything.'

'Yeah?' Escobar's tone said he found difficulty in believing that.

Alvarez left the hotel, crossed to his car and settled behind the wheel, but did not immediately drive off.

After many years, a detective developed an instinctive ability to judge when someone was lying. He had become convinced Short had either been lying or concealing pertinent facts. But because his judgement was based on instinct, it could be very wrong. Perhaps he was allowing his visual opinion of Short to colour his judgement? All the evidence suggested Short had tried to prevent his aunt's going swimming, had become worried, had gone in search of her...

It seemed odd Short had forgotten the name of Lady Gerrard. Titles were relatively rare and what was rare was more readily remembered. Yet why would he lie? Much more reasonable to accept that memory was ever illogical, disappearing when most required, appearing when least wanted ... Two thousand, two hundred and fifty euros was a considerable amount to carry around in cash; a foolish amount. And from the little he had so far learned or discerned, Dora Coates was not a person one would expect to spend anything like that much on holiday. Small points, probably meaningless, yet which nevertheless raised question marks ... He cursed his stupid brain. She had died because she had gone for a swim in the dark, too drunk to save herself when in trouble. What could be more straightforward? Why did he have to manufacture questions which could only cause a great deal of unnecessary work? What perversity of mind prompted him into being unable to accept the obvious?

Seven

'You're very late,' Dolores said, as Alvarez walked into the dining-room.

'I had to question several people and this took longer than I realised.'

'Why were you questioning them?'

'To make certain the English woman died accidentally.'

'But you surely said she'd drowned?'

He crossed to the table, picked up the bottle of Soberano and poured himself a generous brandy, added four cubes of ice. 'One of the easiest ways of concealing murder is by making it appear to be an accident by drowning.'

'You're saying she was murdered?'

'I don't yet know.'

'If you've been questioning people, you must think she might have been.'

'That's enough,' Jaime said.

She was so surprised by her husband's unusual belligerence, it was several seconds before she said, with haughty annoyance:

'Would you like to explain what is enough?'

'You talking about Enrique's work. It's not right for a woman to be interested in such things.'

'You claim to be qualified to decide what a woman may, or may not, be interested in?'

'All I'm saying...'

'Is words made vapid by alcohol.'

'If you're trying to suggest I've drunk too much...'

'Why should I bother when that is so obvious?'

'That's stupid talk.'

'As my mother told me, "A wife must often speak stupidly if she wishes her husband to understand her." '

'Your mother didn't—'

'As far as I can tell,' Alvarez cut in hurriedly, 'the drowning was accidental, but I can't ignore the doctor's evidence.'

'What was that?' she asked, addressing Alvarez, but facing Jaime and silently daring him to complete what he had been going to say.

Alvarez silently sighed with relief when it became obvious Jaime had recovered sufficient sense to say no more. If Dolores became annoyed, her cooking suffered. 'When a person is drowning, she struggles violently before she dies and in the course of her struggles, her fingers can scrape...'

'I don't want to hear any more,' Dolores said. She stood. 'That a man – and of course it was a man – could force such agony on a woman does not surprise me, but it does fill my heart with sorrow.' She crossed to the bead curtain and went through into the kitchen.

Jaime spoke in a low voice. 'She goes on and on to make you tell her and then when you do, won't listen. How the hell do you understand?'

'Only the devil can answer that.'

Alvarez turned into Carrer Grifeu and slowed to read the numbers on the front doors. It was a road of terraced one-floor houses, originally the homes of fishermen and their families, now given a degree of individuality and made cheerful by the different colours in which doors, window frames, and shutters were painted and the window boxes filled with flowering plants. (The influence of foreigners was not all negative.) At the end of the road were several blocks of flats. He could easily remember when none of the houses had been recently painted because no one could afford the luxury of paint, there had been no window boxes because what wife would so publicly admit to wasting time, and beyond had been fields which reached to the mountains.

He opened the front door of No. 21, stepped inside, and called out. An elderly woman who wore widow's black – a custom quickly being lost – entered the front room. He introduced himself and her nervousness was immediate. She had been young in times when the police had to be feared. He dispelled any fears with warm friendliness and explained he wanted a word with Señora Eloísa Cardell. She told him she was Eloísa's mother; her daughter was in her husband's shop where she had to work far too hard because her husband was lazy and spent most of his time in the bars, as all men did. That was, all except officers of the law, she added hastily. Everyone knew they worked tirelessly for the good of everyone. He did not disagree. He asked her where was the shop?

He drove down to the front, turned right. Several hundred metres on, he stopped on a solid yellow line, left the car, and walked into Cardell Treasures. A young assistant whose face he recognised, but whose name he could not remember, said Eloísa was in the office. He walked past tables on which were small leather goods, novelty items –

many of which would not make suitable gifts for maiden aunts – and imitation weapons from the times of El Cid. Items which tourists would buy and on their return home, wonder why. The office was small and very cramped. Eloísa, in her middle thirties, attractive, dressed smartly, faced Alvarez with a self-confidence her mother lacked.

'Is it a good season?' he asked.

She shook her head. 'The tourists look, but don't buy. Perhaps it will improve when the Germans come – they spend more than the British.'

A small man, his face disproportionately featured because of a very high forehead and disrupted by a small and inconsequential moustache, pushed past Alvarez and came to a stop by the desk. 'Where's the box of lambskin slippers?'

'Wherever you left it,' she said wearily.

'Someone wants size thirty-nine and there's none left outside. Find 'em, quick.' He pushed past Alvarez once more as he hurried out.

If that had been Eloísa's husband, Alvarez judged his mother-in-law's criticism to be justified. 'On Tuesday, you told the Policia Local you'd heard a woman shouting at night. Will you tell me about it?'

She spoke rapidly, even for a Mallorquin. She had put her two children to bed, cooked the meal, eaten, tidied up all the things the children had left on the floor, put some clothes in the washing machine, asked her husband to take their dog out for a walk while she washed up – but he had been busy watching the television – had left their house with Carlos – their Ibicencon hound – and taken him to the beach for a quick run. She knew ... Well, she knew one wasn't supposed to take one's dog on to the sand...

He waved aside such bureaucratic nonsense. 'Did you take a torch with you?'

'It wasn't necessary. There wasn't much of a moon, but there was enough light from the road to see where I was going.'

'So what happened on the beach?'

Carlos had run this way and that, as he always did; she'd found a piece of driftwood and thrown it into the sea because he loved swimming and he'd retrieved it and barked for her to throw again. Weary, because there was still work to be done, she'd been about to return home when she'd heard a cry.

Her voice rose. 'If only ... Why was I so stupid as to think...' She became silent, fidgeted with her fingers.

'Señora,' he said quietly, 'we can only do what we think is right at the time. If, later,

92

circumstances suggest it would have been better if we had acted differently, that cannot make us wrong since we do not possess foresight, only hindsight.'

'You really think that's right?'

'I have had to learn it more times than I wish to remember.'

Her fingers became still.

'Tell me about the shouts.'

The woman had cried out in English – she knew some English because it was necessary in her job. She had understood: 'What are you doing? ... Don't ... Please don't.' Then there had been silence. Initially, she had been scared and frightened, but had very quickly had second thoughts. It was a warm night, many couples walked the sand in the dark and then did what couples did. And because she'd heard no more, she'd assumed the woman had decided not to object further.

'So there was no reason to remain alarmed?'

'I didn't think so.'

'What did you do next?'

'God forgive me, I thought that if I continued walking along the beach I would meet them and be so embarrassed that I turned back.'

'Before you did, how far could you see

along the beach?'

'Not very many metres, if you mean to see clearly.'

'But a couple might have been visible at a distance, even if only as dark shadows?'

'I suppose so.'

'You saw no shadows?'

'No.'

'You did not think the cries might have come from the sea?'

'Can't you understand? I was so certain she must be on the beach.'

'Of course I understand that; it's how anyone would have thought. But looking back on things now, do you think the cry might have come from the sea?'

She was silent for a while, her expression bitter. When she did speak, it was in so low a tone he had difficulty in understanding her. 'I can't tell.'

'What was the time when you heard the shouting?'

'I'm not certain.'

'Try to give me a rough idea.'

'I left the house not long after ten thirty.'

'And you heard the shouts how long afterwards?'

'Maybe a little over ten, fifteen minutes. Is ... is that when the English lady drowned?'

'We don't know,' he lied, wanting to leave

her with the chance to hope she had heard not the cry of a woman about to drown, but of a woman who had resisted passion until overwhelmed by it.

Alvarez braked to a halt, shouted through the opened window. The elderly man in the field did not look up and used a mattock to unplug an irrigation channel to allow water to flow between two rows of sweet peppers. Swearing, Alvarez undid the seat-belt, opened the door, stepped out into the sharp sunshine. He shouted again. Was ignored again as the other replugged the one channel, opened the next.

Alvarez walked a few metres to a gate, opened this, went up the field and then across. He recognised Fuentes. 'Are you deaf?'

'Watch where you stick your clodding feet.'

'I'll stick them where I want.'

'In your mouth, most times.' Fuentes straightened up, rested his hands on the end of the haft of the mattock.

Alvarez studied the peppers. 'Don't look so good, do they?'

'They ain't so fat as you, if that's what you means.'

He looked across at the rows of tomatoes.

'They'd likely crop a lot better if you pinched out the side shoots like people do these days.'

'If I wants more bloody stupid advice, I'll ask you,' Fuentes said angrily.

Satisfied he had gained his revenge for being made to leave the car and suffer the short walk in the heat, he said: 'But the beans look as good as any I've seen this year.'

Fuentes grunted.

'Not so many working the fields these days, are there?'

'The young don't want to know what work is.'

'There used not to be a square metre of land that wasn't cultivated; now, field after field is left fallow.'

Fuentes hawked and spat. 'My grandson doesn't know what he wants to do, so I said, take over my land. You'd have thought I was offering him a job cleaning out fosas septicas. Chasing skirt is all he's keen on.'

'In our day, we had to work as well as chase.'

Their brief antagonism – the traditional banter of men of the soil – was lost as they contemplated how the lives of Mallorquins had changed since the tourists had come to the island in their millions.

'I'm looking for an English person, name of Gerrard,' Alvarez finally said.

Fuentes noticed a small clump of newly surfaced weed and used the mattock to dig it out. 'There's two of 'em around here.'

'Husband and wife?'

'Two families. One's in the big house, the other in the caseta up past Ca'n Fyor, not that you'll know where that is.'

'The old mill.'

Fuentes was annoyed.

'Where, I seem to remember, you once worked as look-out.'

'That's daft talk.'

The grinding of corn had been a government monopoly and it had been a criminal offence for any individual to carry out such work without a licence. Mallorquins, never willingly observing the law, had been happy to buy wheat clandestinely milled provided it was cheaper than that on sale in the shops. Ca'n Fyor had served the local area. A spring on top of the hill – no one could offer a reasonable explanation as to why there was a spring at the top when common sense said it should be at the bottom – had been channelled into a holding tank, and when this was full, the water had been released to turn the grinding machinery concealed in a cave in the hillside. The noise of the machinery was considerable, so that when it was operating, there had had to be a look-out – a youngster, reliable but not demanding great rewards. 'They say that much of the contraband which was landed in Cala Tellai used to come past the mill on mules.'

'Folks will say anything that's stupid enough.'

'You never saw a load of cigarettes pass?'

'I'd have spoken up if I had.'

'Now I know you're lying!' Alvarez wished Fuentes good crops, returned to his car.

He drove past Ca'n Fyor – three buildings, one above the other, on the side of the solitary two-hundred-metre hill – to the gently rising land which stretched to the mountains. On his left, twenty metres in from the road, was a caseta and beyond that, visible above pines, were the several roof levels of a large, modern house. Fuentes had said one of the Gerrard families lived in the caseta, but that seemed most unlikely; no English person would live in so mean a building. Fuentes, with true peasant guile, had been making a fool of him.

He parked in front of the caseta, crossed to the front door, knocked. The door was opened by a woman in her middle thirties, attractive rather than pretty because of the considerable character in her face. 'I'm looking for Lady Gerrard,' he said in Mallorquin. 'Can you tell me where she lives?'

She looked at him, her brow furrowed, and it was obvious she was trying to understand what he had said.

'You are English?'

'Yes.'

He translated what he had previously asked her.

'I'm afraid you've come to the wrong house. My sister-in-law lives in Ca'n Jerome.'

'Then I must apologise for troubling you. Perhaps you will tell me how to drive there?'

'It's up the track just past here. But I think she...' She was stopped by a call from behind her. 'Someone wants to talk to Heloise,' she shouted back.

Gerrard entered the sitting-room from the kitchen. 'Would one term that unusual?'

'Not if you were polite. Inspector Alvarez.'

'Cuerpo General de Policia,' Alvarez added.

'A detective?' Gerrard asked.

'Yes, Señor.'

'And you want a word with Heloise. What's she been up to? Cat burglary sounds apposite.'

'For God's sake!' She spoke to Alvarez. 'I have an idea Lady Gerrard is out to lunch.'

'Wasn't it tomorrow she's proving her social flexibility by dining with the Unwins?' Gerrard queried.

'It's easy enough to find out. I'll phone.'

'There's no need to trouble—' Alvarez began. Gerrard interrupted him. 'It's no bother. And whilst you're waiting, we're having drinks so you might like to join us? Or perhaps you're not allowed to drink when on duty?'

'It's left to our discretion.'

'And what is your discretion?'

'It is hot so I should very much like a drink, Señor.'

'Come on in.'

Alvarez, his surprise continuing as he followed Gerrard through a small, dark sitting-room and an equally small, if well-equip- ped, kitchen, to the patio.

'Do sit. What would you like? I can offer gin, whisky, brandy or beer, but I fear we drank the last of the Krug eighty-two last night.'

'May I have a coñac with just ice?'

Gerrard returned into the house and Alvarez settled in a chair. There was an old Mallorquin saw, 'The man who is astonish-ed is fortunate because he has learned something.' To find this English couple living in a small, mean caseta caused him great astonishment, but he wasn't certain where lay the fortune to him.

Gerrard returned, carrying a tray on which were three glasses and a small earthenware bowl filled with crisps. He handed Alvarez a glass, put the other two down on the table together with the bowl, sat.

Laura came out of the house. 'Filipe says Lady Gerrard is out to lunch.'

'Then I must thank you for having saved me a journey, Señora,' Alvarez said.

'Not much of a journey,' Gerrard observed. 'Five hundred metres at the most.' He raised his glass. 'Your good health.'

'And yours, Señor.' Alvarez drank. It was not the quality of brandy one expected in a foreigner's home; indeed, it was no better than he drank in his own. Perhaps this couple were leading a simple life because they found spiritual satisfaction in self-denial. A pleasure he had never understood.

'Since Heloise isn't at home, is there any way in which we can help?' Gerrard asked.

'Is that meant to be a subtle approach?' Laura asked.

'An approach to what?'

'Satisfying your curiosity, because you're forgetting, curiosity is ill manners.'

'You, my love,' Gerrard said lightly, 'are forgetting that curiosity is ill manners in another's house.'

'And this isn't another's house?'

He said nothing.

There had been a sudden bitterness in her voice, Alvarez noted. 'I need to ask Lady Gerrard if two people visited her house.'

'Are we allowed to know their names?' Gerrard asked.

'Señorita Coates and Señor Short.'

'Then I can tell you that they probably did since they called here five, six days ago, thinking this was where she lives. Which points to poor eyesight or lack of common sense. We directed them to Ca'n Jerome.'

'Perhaps you know that Señorita Coates died on Tuesday night?'

'We heard someone of her name had drowned, but we weren't certain if the report was true.'

'It was.'

'Sad.' Gerrard drank, put down his glass. 'There's some problem about her drowning?'

'We have to try to prevent a similar tragedy happening.'

'And Heloise may be able to help you do that?'

'Curiosity killed the...' Laura stopped. 'Not exactly the smartest thing to say, was it? Inspector, do you live locally?'

'In Llueso.'

'Have you always lived in the village?'

'For a long time now, but I was born and lived for several years in another part of the island. My parents had a small farm by the sea.' Which they had been persuaded to sell at a fraction of its later value by a smart con-man. 'And you, Señora, have you been here for many years?'

'It's quite a time. We originally came for three months to find out how Charles liked working here and have just never returned to England. The island has that effect on a number of people.'

'Aeaea,' Gerrard said.

'Does that have meaning or were you clearing your throat?'

'An island of enchantment, lacking only the enchantress, Circe; although the behaviour of some of the tourists can lead one to think she is around.'

'Señor, would you know why Señorita Coates wished to visit Lady Gerrard?'

'I can only guess. She worked for her as a lady's maid until Fergus was born and then as a nursemaid until my nephew required a jailer rather than a nursemaid.'

'A jailer?'

She said: 'As you will probably have gathered, Inspector, my husband has a unique sense of humour – capable of being enjoyed only by himself ... Probably, Dora thought Heloise would be interested to see her and learn what she'd been doing since she left Stayforth House.'

'A totally mistaken belief,' Gerrard said.

'But people quite often like to make contact with someone from their past. Remember how that old gardener turned up for a chat before we left England?'

'Joe? Spent hours talking about late frosts ruining the runner beans and how Father had a guest who ate all the peaches being specially grown for the local flower, fruit, and vegetable show. Couldn't get rid of him.'

'But he got tremendous pleasure from talking to you.'

'Proving that despite Kinsey, pleasure is seldom mutual. I find Dora's visit odd. She's quite sharp enough to know Heloise's forte has never been to reminisce with past employees. And come to that, on my one trip back home, I was at Stayforth and talking to Heloise – can't remember why; arguing over something, probably – when she was told Dora had called to see her. From her reactions, she'd have welcomed Lucrezia Borgia more readily.'

'Señor, would Señorita Coates have been

highly paid?'

'I doubt it, but domestic help has been scare for a long time and so her wages were possibly good. Why do you ask?'

'She had a large sum in her possession. She had also paid for her nephew's holiday.'

'Really? I shouldn't have thought generosity was one of her vices.'

Alvarez drained his glass. 'Thank you for your help, Señor, Señora.'

'You're a one-drink man?' Gerrard asked. 'Or may I refill your glass?'

There was just time for one more drink before he returned home and enjoyed a pre-lunch drink. 'Thank you, Señor.'

Eight

Alvarez had left his office and closed the door when he heard the phone ring. He hesitated. He had been on his way home, but in theory – never mind what he had said to Dolores – he was meant to remain at work until later in the evening. He sighed, opened the door, crossed to the desk, and lifted the receiver. 'Yes?'

'The superior chief wishes to speak to you,' said the secretary with a plum-laden voice.

He went round the desk, phone to ear, sat.

'Why have you not made a report?' Salas demanded, dispensing, as was normal, with any form of social greeting.

'Report about what, Señor?'

'You need to be reminded what cases you are supposed to be investigating? ... Even a modicum of intelligence would enable you to determine that I was referring to the death of Señorita Short.'

'I don't think so, Señor...'

'You are admitting to a lack of even that

106

modicum?'

'It was not Señorita Short who drowned – he is not she and it was she, not he, and so when you said he, but it was she...'

'Do you ever indulge in intelligent speech?'

'Señor Short is alive. It was Señorita Coates who drowned.'

'Which is what I said.'

'No, you said...'

'I'll not have an inspector contradicting me!'

As Claudio Gil had written, 'Injustice is the handmaiden of authority.'

'Have you begun to pursue investigations into the drowning of Señorita Coates? Or, as would seem very likely, are you investigating the death of Señor Short even though he is very much alive?'

'I have questioned Señora Eloísa Cardell, who heard the screams – or shouts. I tried to question Lady Gerrard...'

'You have had the presumption to try to question a lady of quality without any reference to me as to the advisability of your doing any such thing?'

'What her quality is, I don't yet know, not having spoken to her.'

'As a Mallorquin, you are almost certainly incapable of recognising its presence – I don't doubt you would regard someone who knows how to use a knife and fork as being of quality,' Salas said, allowing his resentment over being posted to Mallorca and not to a command on the Peninsula to surface.

'That's ridiculous,' Alvarez said, ever ready to defend his island.

'Your insolence extends to telling your superior officer he is ridiculous?'

'I was referring to the suggestion that we mostly eat with our fingers. To try to eat Sopes Mallorquines, which is a favourite dish, with one's fingers would truly be ridiculous.'

'Stop wasting my time with nonsensical conversation.'

'But, Señor, it was you who said...'

'Was Señorita Coates murdered or did she drown accidentally?'

'It's impossible to be certain at this point.'

'Or probably at any other point, since you are concerned. Have you spoken to the woman who heard the cries?'

'As I said at the beginning, I...'

'Damnit, learn to answer the question.'

'I have spoken to her, yes, Señor. Unfortunately she cannot be certain whether it was a cry of fear or of momentary hesitation.'

'What the devil are you talking about now?'

'As I think I also mentioned before, there has to be the possibility the cry was not made by Señorita Coates, but by a woman who was with a man to whom she had given more encouragement than she had intended...'

'You will refrain from indulging in your perverted interests.'

'She also cannot testify whether the cry came from ashore or the water.'

'Then her evidence is useless.'

'Not completely. I think it points to murder.'

'Then I have little doubt we should assume accidental drowning.'

'If Señorita Coates was murdered, there's the probability Eloísa heard her cry out before her head was finally pushed under the water; the words can support such a picture. The person who pushed probably had to be in water shallow enough to be standing and so gain the necessary leverage; this would be consistent with the evidence of the sand under the finger-nails. Had the drowning been accidental, the cry would surely have been "Help", repeated as often as was possible.'

'Supposition piled on top of supposition. And clearly, being more concerned with possibilities which do not occur to a refined mind, you have not considered that the cry might have been addressed to the fates, not an assailant.'

'I don't understand.'

'I will explain as simply as possible in the hope it will be simple enough. It is a known failing of the human kind to expect life to proceed peacefully – my job constantly proves the falsity of such expectation – and when it does not, a person of weak character blames the fates.'

'If I were drowning, I'd shout for help, not bother about the fates.'

'I am not prepared to accept your reaction as a guide to anything other than mistake. Are you taking any account of the fact she may have been under the influence of alcohol?'

'I've spoken to the hotel staff and established that she was.'

'On your own initiative? ... Then knowing that, does it not occur to you to accept her actions are unlikely to have been logical?'

'I reckon someone who is accidentally drowning will call for help.'

'You are unaware drunken people have drowned in a few inches of water?'

'She wasn't that drunk.'

'A further supposition? Or perhaps a judgement based on experience?'

'If she'd been so totally overcome by alcohol, could she earlier have walked from the hotel to the beach? Yet since she did, surely she must have retained sufficient comprehension to stand up and save herself?'

'Only if in shallow water.'

'The sand under her fingernails says that she was.'

'My understanding is that it proves no more than that she had dug her hands into sand. Drunken people do ridiculous things. Before entering the water, she might well have played in the sand, perhaps making a sand castle.'

'In the dark?'

'You seem determined to treat this as a murder case. Where is the evidence – not supposition – that she did not drown accidentally?'

'There isn't any hard evidence, but instinct tells me she was murdered.'

'Is there a more unreliable gauge? ... What provides the strongest evidence of murder?'

'A body.'

'You like to jest?'

'No, Señor, of course not. It's just that if there isn't a body, one can't be certain of murder unless there is overwhelming circumstantial evidence...'

'Ninety-nine times out of a hundred, there is strong motive for the killing. What motive is there for the Señorita's death?'

'There hasn't been time to...'

'An efficient officer makes time.'

'I was intending to...'

'An inefficient officer always intends to do something, never succeeds in actually doing it.' Salas rang off.

Having replaced the receiver, Alvarez leaned back in the chair. Occasionally, a superior officer said something intelligent. If Dora Coates had been murdered, the prime suspect had to be Short. He knew she had gone swimming, he had left the hotel ostensibly to search for her, making it clear that, as a loving nephew, he was worried on her behalf; he had returned to the hotel and raised the alarm, his wet clothes explained by his having waded into the sea in an attempt to find her. Did he have a motive for her murder? Hatred? Hatred seldom affected only one party, leaving the other unaware of that emotion; she had liked him or she would not have paid for his holiday. Money? For a man who was out of work, two thousand, two hundred and fifty euros in untraceable cash was an appealing sum. But had that cash provided his motive for murder, wouldn't he have taken the money

112

out of her room at the first possible moment, since who would have known it was missing? Or had it been left there because he was clever enough to see the presumption its presence must raise? Perhaps she was quite well off and he was her main or sole beneficiary? The English authorities must be asked to determine her financial position at her death, whether she had left a will and, if so, who were her beneficiaries.

He looked at his watch and was annoyed to learn he could quite properly have left the office a quarter of an hour before.

The steps leading up to the Calvario had been extended, buildings between them and the old square demolished, in order to provide what local authority had considered to be a more impressive approach (one could afford fantasies when the EU was paying the bills). That tradition, the quirks of the past, homes, and memories had been destroyed was of small account.

At eleven fifteen on Friday, Alvarez crossed the old square, from which the Calvario was now visible, and went into Club Llueso for his merienda.

'You're late,' the barman said. 'Thought maybe you wouldn't be coming in here today.'

'Work,' Alvarez answered shortly.

'They say a change is as good as a rest.' He filled a container with coffee, clipped it into the espresso machine. 'So how about a complete change? A coke instead of a brandy with the coffee?'

'You'll never make a living as a comedian.'

The barman picked up a bottle of Soberano and poured out a large drink, slid the glass across. Alvarez lifted it up and drank.

'There's a bloke in *El Dia* saying it'll be the hottest summer the island's ever known,' remarked the barman.

'I've always understood people write in newspapers, not talk.'

'I reckon you won't ever be much of a comedian either.'

Alvarez crossed to one of the window seats. He stared through the window and an overweight woman, wearing straining-tight slacks, went past. Did the foreigners never see themselves as others saw them? There appeared a young woman with raven-black hair, an elfish face, the trimmest of bodies well detailed in hugging-tight blouse and shorts...

'You want to know what frustration is?' the barman asked as he put a cup of coffee down on the table.

'No.'

'It's standing here and watching the likes of her go by outside.'

'I thought you were married?'

'Makes it even more frustrating, doesn't it?'

'But not more than sitting in front of an empty glass.'

As the other, glass in hand, walked away, Alvarez's mind reverted to the problem which was troubling him – did he, or didn't he, bother to seek the superior chief's permission to ask the English authorities for information regarding Dora Coates? Regulations demanded he gain Salas's permission, but to make the request was to give Salas the opportunity to make more irrational and undeserved comments.

The bartender returned and put the refilled glass down on the table. 'A man in Andratx won the primitive lottery this week.'

'Why depress me with someone else's good fortune?'

'You're a miserable old bastard!'

'Not so much of the old.'

'What would you do if you won a really large sum?'

'Move to a village where all the bartenders were dumb,' Alvarez replied, before he picked up the glass and drank.

Nine

Alvarez still had not decided how to forward his request to England; the phone brought a temporary pause to the problem.

'Joaquin Delgado, Institute of Forensic Anatomy. I have the p.m. report on Señorita Coates and thought you'd like a quick résumé.'

Such thoughtfulness momentarily made Alvarez uneasy.

'Death was by drowning in salt water. We have examined the very small incision on the scalp and can offer no definite conclusion, largely because of the time the head was immersed. It could have been inflicted shortly before, but equally feasibly after, the time of death; we cannot be more precise. The possibility that it was caused by a fingernail of someone pressing the head under water has been raised – we can only say size, shape, and depth are all consistent with this possibility, but we cannot determine that that is what happened. We agree with the doctor's judgement that the hands were thrust into sand with considerable force; this is consistent with having occurred during the last convulsive moments before death. There were no signs of drugs, but blood-alcohol level was high; around a hundred and twenty.'

'How drunk did that make her?'

'Can't give you more than a generalisation because each person tends to react differently to the same amount of alcohol; a normally heavy drinker will be affected noticeably less than a light one. This reading falls within the limits of what some mistakenly term "social drinking", the obvious signs of which can be inhibitions lessened, talking volubly or to some extent incoherently, attitude becoming more friendly or more antagonistic than when sober.'

'Could she had reached the stage of drunkenness that when she fell and her head went under water, she just didn't have the instinct to try to save herself by standing up?'

'I shouldn't have thought her instinct of self-preservation had been lost, but as I said earlier, one can seldom be certain to what degree an individual will be affected.'

'I do know she had been drinking heavily during the few days she was on the island.'

'One needs the history of her drinking over a much longer period before drawing any conclusions.'

'It's a very important point of the case.'

'The ones we can't answer so often are.'

It was astonishing how light-heartedly someone would confess ignorance when he didn't have to overcome it, Alvarez thought.

He replaced the receiver. In view of the other's very qualified belief that probably Dora Coates had not been so drunk as to fall down in the water and make no effort to save herself from drowning, the request to the English police for information had become of more importance ... He finally made up his mind, lifted the receiver, dialled.

'Yes?' said the plum-voiced secretary.

'Inspector Alvarez. I'd like to speak to the superior chief.'

'Wait.'

Several minutes later, Salas said: 'Yes?'

'Inspector Alvarez, Señor...'

'Well?'

'I've just received a résumé of the p.m. evidence.' He repeated what he had been told. 'So it seems we should regard murder as more likely than accident, but accept accident as a possibility. Following that...'

'You excel yourself.'

He was gratified Salas should consider his report to be succinct and all-embracing.

'I cannot recall having ever received a more incompetent report.'

He should have remembered the old Mallorquin saying, 'Never sell the calf before the cow has calved.'

'Señor, they were unable to tell me anything more...'

'As you have failed to identify whom or what you are talking about, your report is meaningless.'

'But surely you know that?'

'You believe I am a mind-reader?'

'I hope not.'

'What the devil do you mean by that?'

He hastily tried to cover what he had meant. 'I imagine it could become an unwelcome ability, Señor.'

'It would inevitably lead to utter confusion whenever you were involved ... I find it extraordinary you lack the competence even to understand the necessity of identifying the case, and about whom, you are reporting.'

'I thought it must be obvious.'

'It did not occur to you that at any one moment, I have to consider dozens of cases – thankfully, mostly handled by competent officers?'

'But surely you are not dealing with another case in which a woman was drowned in circumstances which raise the problem of determining whether death was deliberate or accidental?'

'You are trying to be insolent?'

'Of course not.'

'I am to believe your words are no more than thoughtlessness?'

'But how can you ... Señor, I have rung you because I think we need to ask the British police to provide us with any information they can concerning Señorita Coates.'

'Why?'

'Possible motive will be very important.'

'I should be interested to learn what part you believe motive might have played if her death was accidental?'

'What I meant...'

'It might help you to present a lucid report if you could take the trouble to decide just what you do mean before you speak.'

'If we find that were it murder we can identify a motive, then we can accept such motive makes murder more likely.'

'It seems my previous words were far too optimistic. One could well describe what you have just said as illogical incomprehensibility.'

'The obvious possible motives for murdering a middle-aged, physically unattractive woman do not seem to be many so that there has to be a good chance information about her will pinpoint one that is valid. I should like to ask the British authorities to provide us with as wide an evaluation of her background and financial position as possible.'

'Since there is no need to detail the course of your reasons for its being made, I agree.' Salas cut the connection.

Alvarez replaced the receiver, leaned over and opened the bottom right-hand drawer of the desk, brought out a bottle and a glass. He briefly remembered his promise to himself to reduce his drinking, but decided that after a conversation with the superior chief, a brandy became a medical necessity.

He drove past Ca'n Dento, turned left up a wide tarmacked road which ran between fields, stopped in front of Ca'n Jerome. Not unusually, the exterior looked as if the architect – assuming there had been one – had been suffering from some nervous complaint; there were even more roof levels than the eye initially accepted and in addition to this confusion, the portico was of such grand dimensions it was out of proportion

121

to the whole.

He stepped out of the car, briefly stared at the garden and wondered how much it cost to maintain and how much water it consumed, crossed the gravel drive, entered the portico, and pressed the bell to the side of the large wooden door, panelled in a design typical of Granada. The door was opened by Filipe, dressed in white jacket, white shirt and black tie, striped trousers.

Alvarez identified himself. 'I want a word with Lady Gerrard,' he said in Mallorquin.

'Is she in trouble?'

'Not as far as I know.'

Filipe did not try to hide his disappointment. 'You'd better come in.'

Alvarez followed through a couple of rooms as luxuriously furnished as any he had ever seen, out on to the patio. From his experience of wealthy foreigners, he had expected to meet a middle-aged or elderly woman, dowdily dressed, skin wrinkled and shape sagging; he faced a woman in her late twenties or early thirties, dressed with expensive chic, her skin smooth and her shape, as she lay on a chaise longue, exciting to a man of imagination; dark glasses added a hint of hidden delights.

'Is Inspector Alvarez—' Filipe began in English.

She interrupted him. 'How many time have I told you not to bring someone through before you have informed me who has called so that I can decide whether, or not, I am at home?'

'But you is here, Señora.'

'For Heaven's sake, use some intelligence to understand what I'm telling you.'

'Señora,' Alvarez said in English, 'I think he finds difficulty in appreciating the English custom of not being at home when one is at home.'

'Did I ask you?'

'No, Señora.'

'Then there is no need to try to explain. Who are you?'

'Inspector Alvarez of the Cuerpo General de Policia.'

'What do you want?'

'To ask you a few questions.'

'Why?'

'I am conducting an investigation and you may be able to help me. I expect you have heard that most unfortunately an English lady, Señorita—' He was interrupted.

'I'll have some champagne,' she said to Filipe. 'And bring some of those cocktail biscuits. Tell Ana I'll have lunch at half-past one and this time she's to cook the steak better and not try to give me almost raw

123

meat to eat.'

'You tell you like steak raw...'

'Rare. I cannot imagine why I was assured you spoke English well.'

Filipe waited, expecting her to ask Alvarez what he would like to drink. The brandy, Alvarez decided, would be of the finest quality since rich women demanded not only the best for themselves but also for others, since they liked to show their munificence.

'What are you waiting for?' she demanded.

Filipe left.

That she intended to drink, but leave him drinkless, confused Alvarez; there could be no greater measure of rudeness, yet he had given her no cause to be rude.

'How much longer do you intend to stand there?' she asked.

'As I said, Señora...'

'My name is Lady Gerrard.'

'I am sorry, I forgot. We are not used to titles.'

'Naturally, since they are hardly appropriate for you people. Do you intend to explain why you're bothering me?'

'Perhaps you do not know that Señorita Coates very sadly drowned on Tuesday night?'

'Of course I've heard the gossip from

124

people with nothing better to do.'

'I think you may be able to help me in my investigation into her death.'

'Nonsense!'

'Señora ... Lady Gerrard, it is very hot and tiring. Would you mind if I sit?'

'You won't be staying long enough for that.'

'I may well be here for quite some time, so perhaps you won't mind?' Four patio chairs were grouped around a bamboo and glass table and he moved one of them. He was pleased to note her expression of annoyance as he sat. 'There is some difficulty over the facts of Señorita Coates's death...'

'Perhaps you failed to understand me. I am not concerned with her.'

'I understand you met her not long before her death.'

'I did not.'

'My information is she called here to see you...'

'I am not responsible for the misinformation you have been given.'

'She did not come here and speak to you?'

'I have already answered.'

'Is it correct she once worked for you?'

'It's possible.'

'You are not certain?'

'I do not make a point of remembering the

names of all the employees I've had.'

Filipe returned, carrying a silver salver on which was an individual wine cooler in which stood a bottle of Veuve Clicquot and a Waterford crystal bowl containing small Dutch cheese biscuits. He put the salver down on the table, lifted up the bottle.

'Don't shake it,' she snapped.

He removed the foil and found initial difficulty in unwinding the wire.

'Haven't you yet learned how to do that?'

He removed the wire.

'Hold the bottle nearer a glass in case you make a mess of things. For God's sake, why do I have to repeat myself time and again?'

He eased the cork free without losing a drop of champagne and began to pour.

'Not too quickly or it'll come over the top.'

He filled the glass without further instructions, handed it to her; he was about to leave when Alvarez's words, spoke in Mallorquin, checked him.

'Did an English woman come here last Saturday?'

'What are you saying?' Heloise demanded. 'Don't you know it's rude to talk when I can't understand you?'

'Ignore her,' Alvarez said.

'With pleasure, Inspector. Yes, a woman and a man turned up then.'

'Was her name Dora Coates?'

'That's right.'

'What was his name?'

'All I heard was her calling him Colin.'

'Did you learn what the woman wanted?'

'I was told to clear off after I'd asked the Señora if she wanted drinks for them and she'd said she didn't. From the look of her, if she'd given them anything, it would have been arsenic.'

'How long were they here?'

'I couldn't say. She must have let them out.'

Heloise spoke furiously. 'How dare you!'

'Is wrong?' Filipe asked.

'You heard me say you were to speak English, not that awful language I can't understand. Yet you insisted on—'

'No,' Alvarez interrupted, 'I insisted.'

'Just who do you think you are, coming into my house and giving orders to my servant?'

'As a member of the Cuerpo...'

'I don't give a damn what you're a member of.'

'Then perhaps you should start doing so.'

'How dare you speak to me like that. I've never before met such insolence.'

'I am sorry you should think that. I have tried to remain polite.'

'As if any of you know what that word means.' She spoke to Filipe. 'Get on with your job.'

'Perhaps Inspector wish...'

'I don't give a damn what he wants.'

Filipe still did not move.

'It's OK,' Alvarez said. 'I've nothing more to ask you right now.'

Filipe left.

'Lady Gerrard,' Alvarez said, 'when I asked you if Señorita Coates had come here and spoken to you, you said not. But in fact she did.'

'My God, now you are daring to call me a liar!'

'I feel certain you would not lie to a policeman, or to anyone else, so I am sure you just forgot she and a man came here and spoke to you. But since it is important you answer my questions correctly, perhaps you will try to remember exactly what happened.'

She drank avidly, emptying the flute.

The imagined cool, velvet smoothness of some iced brandy became ever more vivid; and as she must be feeling uneasy since he'd exposed her lying ... 'I hesitate to speak, for fear it might be considered ill manners, but it is very hot and I am very thirsty.'

She might have swallowed something

unpleasant before she said: 'Filipe can bring another glass.' She reached out to a bell-push, set in one of the pillars.

'I am afraid I do not greatly like champagne.'

'You think I was going to offer you some? He can get you some beer.'

Filipe came out of the house on to the patio.

'I have been invited to have a drink,' Alvarez told him in Mallorquin before she had a chance to speak.

'What's up with the bitch?'

'She's decided to show the generous side of her nature.'

'If you'd asked me, I'd have said she'd sooner flash her constables at the likes of you and me.'

'Is there some good coñac in the house?'

'Will Bisquit Dubouche be good enough for the grand hidalgo?'

For once his imagination had lagged behind fact. 'Pour a large one and add a couple of cubes of ice.'

Filipe left.

'Lady Gerrard,' Alvarez said, 'it is correct that Señorita Coates came here, isn't it?'

'I forgot.'

'And this was last Saturday?'

'Yes.'

'She was with a companion?'

'Yes.'

'Who was he?'

'Her nephew.'

'What was her reason for coming here?'

'Is that any of your business?'

'I can only say when I know the answer to my question.'

'She mistakenly thought I'd be interested to hear about her life after she left my employment.'

'You were not interested?'

'Of course not.'

'Had you met Señor Short before?'

'No.'

'Then why do you think he came with her?'

'How should I know how their kind think?'

'Were she and her nephew friendly towards each other?'

'Too damned friendly...' She cut short the words.

'You are suggesting their relationship was of an unusual nature?'

'If you are making the disgusting suggestion I think you are, I certainly am not.'

'Then why do you think they were too friendly?'

'Obviously, because she brought him

along.'

Filipe returned, lifted a glass off the salver, and handed it to Alvarez. Even by his own standards, Alvarez acknowledged it was a generous drink. As Filipe returned into the house, Alvarez raised his glass. 'As we say on this island, much happiness.' It was obvious she did not return the spirit of the greeting. He drank. Liquid velvet. If ever he won the lottery he would drink Bisquit Dubouche every morning before lunch. And a glassful in the evening to aid digestion. 'It seems that perhaps their visit disturbed you?'

'Annoyed me. I've better things to do than listen to an ex-employee telling me about her uninteresting life.'

'Did Señorita Coates mention if there were any particular reason for coming here on holiday?'

'No.'

'Might it have been in order to see you?'

'A ridiculous suggestion.'

'Because she would have known you would not welcome her?'

'If she had that much intelligence.'

'Did you meet her again?' It had been a casual, routine question, but he noticed the sudden tightness of her facial muscles. He watched her reach over to the table and fill her glass – pouring too quickly so that

131

foaming champagne spilled over the rim of the glass. It was a pity Filipe could not have seen that. 'When did you see her again?' He spoke as if with the confidence of certainty.

After a while, she muttered: 'Monday.'

'She came here?'

'Yes.'

'Why did she return if she must have known she would not be welcome?'

'Her kind are incapable of appreciating subtleties.'

His glass was empty. He wondered if a gentle hint would cause her to suggest he might like another drink? It seemed too unlikely to be seriously considered. He stood. 'Thank you for your assistance.'

She ignored his thanks.

'I hope I do not have to bother you again.'

She continued to ignore him.

He made his way through the house and as he reached the hall, Filipe appeared through a side doorway. 'Not arresting her?' Filipe asked.

'For what?'

'I can suggest a dozen reasons.'

Ten

On Saturdays – barring an emergency –
Alvarez finished work at lunch time, which
should have meant, with only an hour to
waste before he could leave the office, that
his world was bright and pleasant, but an
unwanted problem was threatening to upset
his peace. He wanted to do his duty, but
there was no point in troubling to draw up a
report if Salas was not in his office to receive
it. Salas very seldom worked on a Saturday;
but might this not be the one when he had
decided to do a little work? And if Salas
somehow learned he had questioned Lady
Gerrard the previous day, but had not
bothered to try to report on the meeting...

He spent time jotting down the points he
wished to make, then dialled.

'The superior chief has had to leave the
office,' said his secretary.

Relief made him light-tongued. 'To play in
a foursome?'

'You mistake insolence for humour.'

133

Salas could not have improved on that. He thanked her for the information, explained why he'd called, rang off.

He walked into the dining/sitting-room, sat down at the table opposite Jaime, brought a glass out of the sideboard and poured himself a brandy, added four cubes of ice. Jaime leaned forward and spoke in a low voice. 'She's been singing.'

Dolores's songs expressed both her pleasure and her displeasure; they foretold a meal of ambrosia or meal of badly cooked chickpeas. 'Was it the song about the man who deserts his childhood sweetheart for a tart in Madrid?'

'No. Haven't heard this one before. Seemed to be about love resembling two nightingales. Real daft! Like two nightingales!'

Alvarez decided it would lead to too many complications to try to explain to Jaime that probably the words were loosely based on the nineteenth-century poem by Cañellas in which nightingales were compared with true love because they paired for life and their songs sweetened all those who heard them. He drank. Since Dolores seemed to be in a good mood, she might be preparing Guattleras amb figes. He could almost taste the quail cooked with herbs, onions, white wine, bitter chocolate, and figs.

Dolores came through the bead curtain. 'Where are the children?'

'I haven't seen 'em,' Jaime replied.

'Then will you find them and say lunch will be in fifteen minutes and they're not to be late or the meal will be ruined.' She returned to the kitchen.

'D'you get that?' Jaime asked excitedly. 'Never went at me for not knowing where they are!' He drained his glass, refilled it. 'Maybe some relative has died and left her a fortune.'

'Has she one likely to leave anything but debts?'

Jaime drank. 'Gilberto, who went out to Chile, always had a soft spot for her and I've been told he's done very well for himself.'

'He'll have married.'

'She could have died first.'

'There'll be children.'

'Maybe she couldn't have any.'

'It's an empty purse that's filled with other people's money.'

'Sometimes you talk real daft! Why suddenly go on about empty purses?'

'Have you forgotten she asked you to find Isabel and Juan?'

'So why's she on at me like that? A man

sits down to rest after working real hard and all the wife can say is, do this, do that.' He drained his glass. 'Have you seen 'em recently?'

'No.'

'You wouldn't like to go out and look for 'em.'

'You're right, I wouldn't.'

There was a call from the kitchen. 'Are the children in?'

'Jaime's gone looking for them,' Alvarez replied, as Jaime came to his feet and hurriedly left the room.

Dolores came through the bead curtain. 'I told them not to go far away as I didn't want the meal to spoil. But children will be children, won't they?'

'So people say,' Alvarez replied.

'And where would we be without them? How much richer life is when one has children.'

His impression was, one's life became much poorer since children were so demanding.

'To see them grow and succeed in life is the finest gift a person can have.' She returned to the kitchen.

He wondered uneasily what had caused her to talk in such terms.

When all were at table, she served Coliflor

al estilo de Badajoz. As delicious as were the florets of cauliflower fried in egg and breadcrumbs, Alvarez could not forget his imagined Guattleras amb figes...

Dolores, helped by Isabel, cleared the plates and put on the table bananas and baked almonds. They ate, largely in silence, before Dolores said: 'You'll never guess who I met this morning.'

Juan said: 'Can we get down from table?'

'Before most of us have finished eating?'

'He wants to see Carolina,' Isabel said spitefully.

'No, I don't.'

'Yes, you do.'

'No, I don't.'

'You want to mush her again. You thought me and Inés couldn't see, didn't you?'

'You...' Juan used a fanciful Mallorquin expression.

'How dare you!' Dolores snapped.

'But she and Inés were peeking.'

'If I ever hear you speak such language again, I'll wash your mouth out with soap.'

'Do you know what she called me yesterday?'

'I am not interested.'

'She called me a...' Juan spoke a second and equally fanciful Mallorquin expression.

'I did not,' Isabel protested shrilly.

'Get down from the table, both of you, before I send you up to your bedrooms,' Dolores snapped.

They hurriedly left.

'Of course,' she said, each word spoken with sharpened edges, 'you understand why they speak such disgusting things. It is because they so often hear them in this house, they mistakenly believe them to be harmless.'

'I've never said anything like that here,' Jaime protested. Then he added: 'Or in any other house.'

She ate an almond with unnecessary vigour. 'As my mother used to say, "A man will stand in the rain and swear it is sunny." ' After a moment, she asked: 'What does "mush" mean?'

'It's just kids' talk,' Jaime answered.

She ate some banana. 'If I thought Juan and Carolina could be...' She did not finish.

'They're not going to get up to fun and games at their age.'

'How typical! Has there ever lived a man who has considered that his fun and games become a woman's pain and misery? Of course not! A man considers only himself.' She ate the last almond on her plate, stood. 'I will clear the table since it would be a waste of breath to ask either of you to do that to save me a little work.'

'No more singing,' Jaime said in a low voice as she went into the kitchen.

She came through the bead curtain and stopped by the table. 'You can pour me a small coñac when you give yourselves one and I'll drink it after I've cleared the table and before I wash up.' She picked up the serving dish and two glasses, carried them through to the kitchen.

Jaime opened the nearer sideboard door, but did not reach inside. 'Do you reckon she's all right?'

'There's nothing obviously wrong,' Alvarez replied.

'But it's just not like her, saying we'll all have a coñac instead of going on at us because that's what we're doing.'

'Never question good fortune for fear it will leave more quickly than it arrived.'

Jaime brought an unopened bottle of Fundador out of the sideboard, unscrewed the cap, poured out three brandies. After passing one glass to Alvarez, pushing a second one across to Dolores's place, he raised his and drank. He looked at the bead curtain and topped up his glass.

Dolores returned and sat, warmed the glass in her hand. 'I was going to tell you who I met this morning. Benito Ortega with

Luisa and Ana. They were very friendly.'

'Must have wanted to borrow something,' Jaime said.

'You talk absurdities. What should a man who has just bought Son Estar wish to borrow from me?'

'The money to pay for it.'

'As if I could give him enough for even a square metre of so grand a house! Luisa told me they were having the decoration and furnishing carried out by firms in Palma. What will that cost?'

'Whatever it does, it'll be paid for in fool's money.'

'She was wearing a dress that cost more than I spend on clothes in a year and her jewellery was not the same as the last time we met; she must have more jewels than the Queen.' She drank. 'I have asked them to a meal.'

'You've what?'

'You are surprised I should ask old friends here?'

'They were never friends, not with him always on the scrounge and her like month-old milk. The daughter will be even worse. They always are.'

'You speak from personal experience?' Dolores asked sharply. She finished her drink, stood. 'The bottle can go back.'

'I'll do that in a minute,' Jaime said.

'Now!'

She watched him return the bottle to the sideboard, then went into the kitchen.

Could a chameleon begin to change its colours as quickly as a woman her moods? Alvarez wondered. Almost between sentences, Dolores's mood had changed from sunny to stormy. Just for once, of course, he probably knew why. Married women saw it as their duty to find wives for unmarried men and she had decided Eva was to be his. Could she really think any fortune would compensate for marriage to the daughter of Luisa Ortega?

Eleven

When the universe was created, so were certainties. There could be no light without darkness, good without evil, birth without death, Sundays not followed by Mondays. Alvarez sat at his desk and gloomily faced five and a half working days.

He lit a cigarette before he remembered his resolution to cut back on his smoking. He stared at the unopened mail and, because of his sombre mood, became certain one of the five letters would call on him to take some action that was impossible, inadvisable, illogical, or disruptive.

The door opened and a cabo entered. 'Never seen a guy work as hard as you do.'

'You want something?' he asked coldly.

'If I did, I wouldn't waste time here ... This has just come through.' The cabo held out three sheets of paper.

'What's it about?'

'Maybe you'll find out if you can read.' The cabo put the faxed message down on the desk, left.

Alvarez read the report from the English police. Dora Anne Coates, aged 62, had lived in a bungalow on the outskirts of Tonbridge. No criminal record. She had retired from domestic service some years before. Neighbours described her as a withdrawn, largely friendless woman who lived a quiet life. She had made a will two years previously and this left a thousand pounds and the contents of her bungalow to her nephew, Colin John Short, and the remainder of her estate to Charles Chauncy Gerrard. At the time of her death, she had a bank account in which were seven hundred and fifty-two pounds and a building society account in which were eighty-one thousand, five hundred and twenty-one pounds; the bungalow was valued at one hundred and twenty thousand pounds.

Alvarez leaned back in the chair. Her savings suggested she had had no need to lead a frugal life, but elderly persons often suffered unwarranted fears of poverty. Someone who came to the island with over two thousand euros in cash could hardly be described as holidaying frugally. He wondered if there were any significance in this contradiction, decided it was merely one more indication of human illogicality. Far

143

more important was the fact that if Dora Coates had been murdered, money provided the possible motive and on only this basis, one person was brought sharply into focus – Gerrard – and one person could be virtually eliminated – Short – unless the contents of the bungalow were very valuable, which seemed unlikely as there had been no suggestion of this in the report.

Two hundred thousand pounds was very roughly thirty-five million pesetas (he still could not judge comparative values in euros; probably never would be able to), which was a fortune. Many a murder was committed for much less. Yet despite the obvious evidence of a lack of money, he would judge Gerrard to be a man for whom no fortune would be sufficient to tempt him willingly to hurt an elderly woman. Could such judgement be so very wrong? Could money, and the lack of it, corrupt anyone?

The Gerrards were not at home. Alvarez returned to his car and settled behind the wheel. He could stay where he was, in the hope they had not gone away for long – but the sun was hot and the interior of the car was becoming like a fired boiler despite the lowered windows. He could return to the office – but there, he was a hostage to trouble.

A BMW, in which he recognised Heloise in the back, drove up. The driving door opened, Filipe stepped out and crossed to the Ibiza. 'I said it was you, Inspector, only she insisted it wasn't.'

'Then I can't possibly be me.'

'Is Señor Gerrard in the house?'

'It doesn't seem so.'

'I'll tell her and likely be blamed for not knocking properly or ringing the wrong bell.'

'She can always get out of the car and check for herself.'

'You believe in miracles? Got to take her into Palma to a dress shop and she'll be in there for hours. We could live like kings on what she spends on clothes.'

The rear window of the BMW slid down. 'What are you doing?' Heloise demanded.

'I speak Inspector.'

'Are they or aren't they at home?'

'You pardon?'

'Why the hell do I put up with someone so stupid? Is Mr Gerrard in the house?'

Alvarez answered her. 'Neither Mr nor Mrs Gerrard is at home, Lady Gerrard.'

'I don't remember asking you.' The window rose.

'What did you say to annoy her?' Filipe asked.

'Just tried to help.'

Heloise's shrill voice interrupted their conversation. 'Will you kindly take me to Palma instead of wasting time.'

'I do.' Filipe returned to the BMW, drove off.

Since she would be in Palma, Alvarez decided it would be a good moment to speak to Ana. He drove the short, looped route to Ca'n Jerome.

Ana, not young but still a useful way away from middle age, opened the front door. He introduced himself, said he'd just spoken to Filipe, and explained he would like a word with her; noticing her uneasiness, he added that there was absolutely no need for her to be worried, it was simply that she might be able to help him in his inquiry into the drowning. Of course he realised she had never met Señorita Coates and so couldn't in any way be connected with the tragedy, but ... He could project a warm charm which quickly put at ease a nervous person. Only minutes after first speaking to her, she offered him coffee.

He sat in the small alcove in the kitchen and as she prepared the coffee, surveyed the electrical equipment. Wealth allowed one to

146

buy all manner of labour-saving machines; great wealth, the ability to hire labour to work those machines. The espresso machine hissed and two cups filled with coffee; she put these on the table, together with a small jug of milk and a bowl of brown sugar. 'Maybe you'd like a coñac with the coffee?'

'Just for once, I think I would.'

'The Señora – that's what I like to call her when she can't hear me – gives us a bottle now and then.'

'And so she should.' Remembering Heloise's character, it seemed unlikely she was so generous, but if Filipe and Ana helped themselves – and their guests – from time to time, what harm was done?

Ana put a bottle of Hors d'age on the table together with one glass. As good as that brandy was, he knew a moment's disappointment that she had not chosen Bisquit Dubouche. 'Aren't you having a drink?'

She shook her head. 'I don't really like it.' She spooned sugar into her cup, stirred with nervous energy. 'I still don't understand why you think I can help?'

'To tell the truth, it's likely you can't, but there is just the chance you can tell me something useful ... Is it right that Señorita Coates came twice to the house?'

She nodded.

147

'Was Lady Gerrard pleased to see her?'

'Not according to Filipe. Each time, he reckoned she'd have liked to have had them thrown out. And that first time, after they'd gone, she was in a really bad mood. Told me the meal I'd cooked was terrible. It wasn't. I'd taken a lot of trouble preparing it and it was really tasty.'

'What had you cooked? Ternasco asado?' Who could accurately describe the pleasure of roast baby lamb cooked with white wine, lemon, garlic...

'She won't touch any Spanish dishes; everything has to be like it is in England.'

'That's probably why she's so sour.'

She smiled briefly. He drank some brandy, poured what was left into the coffee. 'So it looked like their turning up got her into a really bad mood?'

'Could have been that; could have been anything. She'll start shouting at us if something goes wrong, even if it's her own fault.'

'So neither you nor Filipe had any idea what really upset her?'

'Not that time.'

'You maybe did when they came the second time?'

'It's just...' She stopped.

'Tell me.'

'Filipe heard them shouting at each other.

He knows English better than he speaks it, but they were talking real fast so he only understood some of the words, but he was certain the Señora and the man were threatening each other.'

'Did he gather what the threats were about?'

'No. But he told me he'd never heard the Señora sounding so bitchy and that's saying something, I can tell you!'

'You're being very helpful.'

'Am I?'

'Indeed.' He absentmindedly refilled his glass. 'I've been told Señor Gerrard who lives in Ca'n Dento is Lady Gerrard's brother-in-law, but can that be right? They have the same name, but she lives here and must have more money than one dreams about and he lives in a caseta and probably has as much difficulty in paying the bills as you and me.'

'He is her brother-in-law. He's poor because he's an author.'

'That makes sense. But it's strange seeing two branches of a family living at such different levels.'

'You wouldn't expect her to help them out, would you?'

'Surely she might?'

'You obviously don't understand what

149

kind of a woman she is. They came for a meal not so long ago. Like I told you, Filipe understands English better than he speaks only she doesn't believe he does, so sometimes he hears things which he wouldn't if she knew – she'd order him away. She told Señor Gerrard she was going to start charging rent for Ca'n Dento.'

'The caseta belongs to her?'

'If she's going to make them pay, it must do.'

'If the Señor's hard up, it seems a nasty thing to do when it'll mean much to him and little to her.'

'That's only the half of it. Señor Gerrard has a son and she told him she wouldn't pay for the school any longer ... Do people have to pay in England?'

'If they send their children to a public school.'

'But if it's public, it must surely be free?'

'In England, public means private.'

'It must be a very strange language.'

'They are very strange people ... So the Señora was making their financial lives very difficult?'

'And enjoyed doing so, like as not. Because of how she is, Filipe and me would be looking for another job if she didn't...'

'Pay so well?'

'Her? Like all the rich, she guards the euros. It's just she spends time in England where she owns a big house and when she's not here, life is not so difficult. It's not that we're lazy,' she added hurriedly, 'but it's nice to be able to take life a little more easily sometimes.'

'I know just what you mean,' he assured her.

He turned on to the road and drove towards Llueso. It seemed Lady Gerrard's vindictiveness was going to make Gerrard's life, already hard, much harder. Two hundred thousand pounds would not only remove that threat, the money would provide a degree of financial safety for the family, a goal most husbands and fathers would seek at almost any cost.

Twelve

Alvarez entered the foyer of Hotel Monterray and crossed to the reception desk.

'Back to ask more unimportant questions?' Bonet asked sarcastically.

'To have a word with Señor Short.'

'If you're not careful, he'll begin to think you have suspicions.'

'And if you're not careful, you'll find yourself wishing you'd minded your own affairs instead of other people's.'

'That's typical – pass an amusing comment and you immediately take offence. You blokes just don't have any sense of humour.'

'We just laugh at different things. Is he in his room?'

Bonet looked round at the key board. 'No.'

'Where d'you think he is?'

'Likely on the beach with the woman he's been chasing since she arrived.'

Alvarez returned outside, crossed the pedestrianised area, and began to walk along the beach. Within a minute, he saw

Short in the company of a topless blonde. As he approached, he tried not to appreciate her generous breasts; that was difficult.

Short looked up, squinting to protect his eyes from the glare of the sun which, although dipping down towards the mountains, was still fiercely bright. 'What the hell do you want this time?'

'A word or two.'

'You can't see it's not convenient?'

Alvarez wondered if she had had a breast implant or nature had been generous.

'Who is it?' she asked.

'A detective.'

'Has something happened?'

'It'll be about Dora.' He spoke to Alvarez. 'Suppose you come back tomorrow?'

'I'm afraid I must speak to you now.'

'Then it's your bad luck because I'm not moving.'

'You musn't talk to him like that,' she said nervously.

'Why not?'

'Because it's silly to cause trouble.'

'I'm not going to be ordered about by some self-important copper.'

'Colin, you can't say that sort of thing here. You've got to be so careful – the police are much tougher than at home.'

'But we seldom shoot people on a Monday,' Alvarez said, to prove he had a good sense of humour.

She stood up so quickly, her breasts – as Alvarez inadvertently observed – jiggled. 'For God's sake do as he wants. Look, I'll see you later.' She hurriedly put on a bikini top, picked up a towel, and left, eager to escape trouble.

'It will be best, I think, if we return to the hotel to speak,' Alvarez said.

'You do, do you?' Short spoke in tones of confrontation, but he stood, pushed his feet into slip-slops.

In the hotel, Alvarez asked: 'Is the office free for our chat?'

'I guess,' Bonet answered. 'And would there be anything more Don Alvarez requires?'

'Just the usual.'

In the office, Alvarez sat behind the desk, Short in front. 'I'm sorry to have had to ask you to leave the beach,' Alvarez said formally.

'Must have made you bloody well weep!'

'It was necessary because I have received information from England.'

'Yeah?' Short spoke with careless uninterest.

'Señora Coates has left a will. Do you know what are the contents of that?'

'Didn't know she'd made one.'

'You are one of the beneficiaries. You are to inherit a thousand pounds and the contents of her bungalow.'

Short laughed sarcastically.

'Why does that amuse you?'

'Because what's in the bungalow wouldn't interest a rag-and-bone man.'

'There is no valuable furniture?'

'Never been in a place where a spinster's lived for years? It's filled with junk and the smell of stale lavender.'

'I understand that the bungalow is valued at a hundred and twenty thousand pounds.'

'It'll need a mug to pay that sort of money.'

'She had a bank account in which was over seven hundred pounds and a building society account with over eighty thousand pounds.'

'Almost a capitalist!'

'It doesn't surprise you she possessed so much?'

'The last person she worked for was an old man whose wife had died; he became weak and she wanted to quit because he needed so much done for him, but he promised that if she'd stay, he'd leave her everything he had.'

'You think she was able to buy the bungalow and have that much money in her accounts because of what she had inherited from him?'

'Must have been.'

The door opened and a waiter came in. 'Sorry it's taken a bit of time.' He handed a glass to Alvarez, turned to Short. 'You want something?' he asked in English.

'Not right now.'

The waiter left.

Alvarez fidgeted with the glass to send the four ice cubes circling the brandy. 'Were you her nearest living relative?'

'Unless there's a little bastard tucked away somewhere.'

'Then it must be disappointing that she has not left everything to you.'

'I could have done with it, sure, but it was up to her. What did she do – leave it to a cat's home?'

'To Señor Gerrard.'

Short's astonishment was obvious. 'You're having me on.'

'That is what England has told me.'

'She must have been losing her marbles when she made the will.'

'Why do you say that?'

'She'd worked for the family, hadn't she? Always said that when she was in service, the wives were usually bitches and Lady

Gerrard was the biggest bitch of the lot.'

'Is it likely she ever worked for Señora Gerrard?'

'If one member of the family gets up your nose, you don't usually stop to think that maybe the others won't.'

'Is it possible Señor Gerrard was embarrassed to see how she was treated when she worked for Lady Gerrard and so went out of his way to be kind to her; she remembered this with such gratitude, she made him her heir?'

'I wouldn't know. But if that's the way it was, good luck to him.'

Alvarez was pleasantly surprised by Short's attitude; there were many who would not have accepted 'disinheritance' so philosophically. Confirmation that one should not condemn modern youth simply because they lacked so many of the visible qualities good taste demanded.

'You are very silent, Enrique,' Dolores said, as she looked at Alvarez across the dining-room table.

'Why complain?' Jaime asked.

'Because when he is silent, you are given an opportunity to speak,' she snapped.

Jaime emptied his glass and then, in a rare moment of rebellion, refilled it despite the fact she was watching.

'You are well?' she asked Alvarez.

'Never felt better. It's just I've been wondering if there's anyone else on the island who could serve Huevos serranos which tasted even half as good as the ones we've just eaten.'

She doubted his words whilst not denying he was right. 'My mother taught me because she always said the most important thing for a wife to know was how to cook meals her husband would appreciate—'

Jaime interrupted her. 'She got that right!'

'...because a man with a full belly is less trouble than a man with an empty one.'

'Your father must have eaten very well.'

'You wish to suggest that this is because otherwise he would have caused so much trouble?'

'Why do you twist everything I say?'

'If you drank less, you might understand it is only in your mind that my words become twisted.'

'I've hardly had anything this meal.'

'Then I am surprised there should be two empty bottles on the table.'

'Because the first was almost empty at the start of the meal. And I haven't drunk it all – what about Enrique? He's had glass for glass.'

'I hope that soon he may be more fortunate than you and marry a woman who is not so indulgent as I. She will persuade him of the joys of self-restraint.'

'More likely drive him into being a five-bottle man if her name's Eva,' Alvarez said.

She stood. 'A woman dedicates herself to serve the men in her lives. Poor deluded fools that we are! Sooner pet a hungry lion than expect a man to appreciate our sacrifices.' She pushed back her chair, stood, marched through to the kitchen.

'You've put her into a foul mood!' Jaime said resentfully.

'Self-preservation,' Alvarez replied.

Thirteen

As Alvarez drove slowly towards Ca'n Dento, he tried to marshal his thoughts. Charles and Laura Gerrard were far from being financially secure – indeed, they were probably amongst the poorest of the foreign residents. Yet even their low standard of living had been threatened when his sister-in-law had told them she intended to charge them rent and they would have to pay their son's school fees. When a man saw his family face disaster, he fought; fought with every means at hand, careless if someone else was hurt. But surely 'character' must delineate what 'means' were to hand? One man might not bring himself to steal, another might readily turn to murder...

Many would laugh at such an old-fashioned concept, but he judged Charles Gerrard, despite the fact he was an author, to be the epitome of the traditional English gentleman – totally honest, always courteous and considerate towards others, never willingly harming anything but foxes and game in season. Would such a man betray his character? Would he accept murder as the only way of protecting his family?

How could Gerrard have known he was the main beneficiary in Dora Coates's will – necessary if he had committed murder in order to benefit from her death? Might she have told him its contents in order to enjoy his surprised gratitude? Why had she left almost everything to him and very little to her nephew?

He parked in front of the caseta, crossed to the front door, and knocked. Time bred paradoxes. Many decades ago, this caseta in good condition would have signalled that the occupants were as well off as most; now, especially for a foreigner, it was a badge of hardship.

Laura opened the door. 'Inspector!' The single word was both greeting and question.

'I am sorry to trouble you again, Señora Gerrard, but I need to speak to you and the Señor.'

'Then come on in. It really is hot today, isn't it? We were talking to a man herding some goats and he said – that is, I think it's what he said because he could only speak Mallorquin – it's the hottest May anyone's known.'

161

'I think he has to be right.' He stepped into the sitting-room. Pedants would decry the possibility a room could express emotion, but for him this one spoke of quiet happiness. He hoped he would not have to destroy that.

He followed her through the kitchen and out to the vine-covered patio.

'Hullo, there,' Gerrard said, as he came to his feet. 'Is it good fortune or careful planning?'

'Señor?'

'Sooner or later,' she said, 'I always have to apologise for my husband.'

'I am afraid I do not understand.'

'Just before you arrived, Charles decided the sun was over the yardarm – his yardarm, needless to say – and therefore it was time for drinks. I hope you won't allow his ill-chosen words to prevent your joining us?'

'I should be happy not to.'

'After working that out,' Gerrard said, 'I think it's in order to ask you what you'd like to drink?'

'A coñac with just ice, please.'

'I'll get them,' she said, then returned into the house.

Gerrard waited until Alvarez had sat on the opposite side of the patio table before he said: 'Presumably, you're here again on account of Dora's death?'

'That is so.'

'Because there is a problem.'

'It is too early to answer precisely.'

'He who prevaricates, asserts.'

'There are one or two points we still have to clarify.'

'Which translated means, you are now convinced her death was not accidental.'

'On the contrary, we are still not certain.'

'The more forcibly authority denies, the more certain one has heard the truth ... Why do you think we may be able to help you?'

'You knew Señorita Coates when you lived in England.'

'To "know" has many meanings, one of which – the biblical sense – is sufficiently unlikely as to be ignored.'

'Did you often meet her when she was working for your brother?'

'Not often, since my sister-in-law has always frowned on staff mixing with guests.'

'Did you find the Señorita an interesting person?'

'I don't think I would have described her in quite that way.'

'You got on well with her?'

'In what sense?'

'As you have told me, Lady Gerrard had a certain attitude towards staff; did you have a different one, did you treat Señorita Coates with obvious friendliness?'

'I hope I'm always friendly to someone who's not given me cause to be unfriendly. Just why are you asking these questions...' He stopped as Laura came out of the house, a tray in her hands. She handed out the glasses, put the tray on the ground, sat.

Gerrard raised his glass. 'Good health ... The Inspector says Dora probably did not drown accidentally, but was murdered.'

Laura, who had been about to drink, said 'Oh!', held the glass in front of her mouth.

'No, Señor, I did not say that,' Alvarez corrected. 'I explained I am here because there are one or two matters concerning the Señorita's death which still have to be clarified.'

'And you think we can help you do that?' She finally drank, put the glass down on the table.

'It is possible, Señora.'

'But we only ever met her before we came out here when we were at Stayforth House.'

'Yet when you did meet her, you were friendly?'

'Of course. Why do you ask?'

'You will understand in a minute, Señora.'

'That seems an optimistic prediction,' Gerrard observed.

'Perhaps more friendly to her than to others?'

'I don't know how one would describe it. We did make a point of always talking to her and asking her how she was.'

Gerrard said: 'Inspector, you appear to be a very straightforward person, which means you are full of guile. So you have a reason for believing the relationship between Dora and us might have some bearing on her death. Isn't it time to explain why?'

'I have to explore every possibility, Señor.'

'Blind alleys lead nowhere.'

'Would you imagine she possessed much of value when she died?'

'She can't have saved much on her wages and I imagine her only other asset was the state pension.'

'She owned a bungalow which has been valued at a hundred and twenty thousand pounds and a building society and bank account in which are over eighty thousand pounds.'

'Well, I'll be damned! ... Where on earth did all that come from?'

'It seems she was left money by an employer.'

'I'm glad to hear that in her retirement she was able to lead a far more comfortable life than she probably expected. Tragic she should die as she did.'

'Would you know who was her heir?'

'Her nephew, presumably.'

'She left him very little.'

'That's odd, since she seems to have been fond of him; must have been, to bring him on holiday.'

'Her heir, Señor, is you.'

'That's ridiculous!'

'My information comes from the English police.'

'Even so, there has to be a mistake.'

'I doubt that.'

'Why would she leave me a penny?'

'Perhaps because you and the Señora took the trouble to be friendly when at your brother's home.'

'All we ever did was have a bit of a chat and a laugh.'

'If a person is unhappy and alone, treated without sympathy, perhaps even with contempt, any sign of friendship can be very treasured.'

'But...'

'You had no idea she had named you her heir?'

'How on earth could I? If you'd asked me, I'd have said – as I did just now – that if she had anything much to leave, it would all go to her nephew ... Frankly, even if it was the police who told you this, I think it's a ridiculous mistake.'

There was a brief silence.

'Señor, I have to ask some questions which may seem strange.'

'After what you've just told us, brillig and slithy toves are models of normalcy.'

'Would you describe yourself as financially secure?'

'My sense of humour doesn't stretch that far.'

'And you have in the past been helped financially by your sister-in-law?'

'No,' Laura said sharply, 'by his brother.'

'What has any of this to do with you?' Gerrard demanded, embarrassment fuelling sudden annoyance.

'I regret, but I have to know.'

'You're investigating Dora's death, not my finances.'

'Have you been living here without paying rent to Lady Gerrard who owns the property?'

After a long while, Gerrard muttered: 'Yes.'

Laura said; 'Jerome, not the family trust, bought Ca'n Plomo and Ca'n Dento and he suggested Charles tried living here to find out if the ambience helped his writing. Naturally, we offered to pay rent, but

167

Jerome refused and told us we could live here for as long as we wanted, rent free.'

'But that has changed?'

'My sister-in-law,' she replied, tone expressing what she did not put into words, 'has decided she needs to increase her income to match her spending. One way of doing that, while at the same time getting her own back...'

'Steady on,' Gerrard said.

'You know as well as I that the rent means nothing to her; the attraction is the vindictive pleasure of knowing she's making your life more difficult.'

'Why should she wish to do that, Señora?' Alvarez asked.

'Because she's never understood she's hopelessly wrong about Charles. He does not look down on her because of her background. She cannot understand that he judges everyone on who they are, not where they've come from—'

Gerrard interrupted her. 'I don't think you're being fair.'

'Because you're too reluctant to believe the worst, because you're concerned about keeping family matters within the family. But the Inspector asked a question because he wants to know what the relationship was and is. You can't deny Jerome always did his best to make up for what he had and you didn't, whereas she loves to flaunt the difference.'

'Vive la différence and let it all hang out.'

'Stop trying to use humour to conceal your feelings.'

'Thank you for those few kind words.'

'Señora, when you say your brother-in-law made up for what he had and your husband did not, what exactly does that mean?'

'The English law of primogeniture. It keeps large estates intact, but means the elder brother inherits everything and the younger brother nothing. When he was alive, Jerome helped him as much as the trust allowed him to; after he died, Heloise has made certain Charles is on his own.'

'To the extent that she is also asking you to pay the fees at the school at which your son studies?'

Gerrard said sharply: 'How do you know that?'

'Is it true?'

'Yes. And I'll ask again, how do you know that?'

'Señor, you must understand that the source of a policeman's information has to remain confidential.'

'But not unidentifiable. We were given the news when we had a meal with Heloise.

Presumably, Filipe, whom I've always guessed understood far more English than was apparent or she accepted, passed on the information to you?'

Alvarez did not answer.

'And you are asking questions which on the face of things can have no connection with Dora's death because you believe that in truth they may be very pertinent as well as impertinent?'

'Charles,' she said, 'how on earth can paying rent or school fees possibly have anything to do with Dora?'

'Remember what the Inspector told us earlier about the will. We are facing financial meltdown, since having paid the rent, even if we give up eating and drinking, there's no way in which we'll be able to afford the fees at Barnsford Close. So...'

'So what?'

'If a small fortune were suddenly to arrive out of the blue sea, all our problems would be solved.'

'Surely to God you're not suggesting...'

'I am not, but like the queen, the Inspector is capable of believing one impossible thing after breakfast, as well as six before.'

She spoke shrilly. 'Do you have to go on and on talking nonsense?'

'How else to calm my nerves? And

beneath the nonsense is, I promise you, hard sense ... Let the Inspector prove my point. Inspector, are you not trying to determine whether or not I might have killed Dora?'

'Señor, as I have said, I am doing no more than examining all possibilities.'

'And I provide a very interesting one?'

She faced Alvarez, her expression drawn tight from panicky anger. 'How can you begin to think Charles could do so terrible a thing?'

'Señora, I have not said that I do.'

She turned to her husband. 'Then for God's sake, stop it.'

'As was said by an Irishman after visiting a Trappist monastery, "The truth is spoken in the unspoken words." ... Inspector, why do you consider me a prime suspect?'

'As I said to the Señora...'

'We are now discussing what you didn't say.'

'I find that difficult.'

'But far from impossible if one uses a little logical imagination. If we were one small step from bankruptcy, Dora's extraordinary bequest meant our financial problems could disappear as quickly as snow in the Sahara. True. But such projection raises a problem. How could I know the details of her will?

Do you have an answer?'

'If I also may employ a little imagination, at some time in the past, she told you what she intended.'

'Why should she do that?'

'To express her thanks for your wife's and your past friendliness.'

'I would never say she was a woman to value the past.'

'Then to enjoy the pleasure gained from your gratitude.'

'She found it difficult to enjoy her own pleasure, let alone anyone else's.'

'Perhaps her motive was less honourable than we're allowing – her pleasure relied on knowing you would be beholden to her.'

'Far too subtle for a straightforward, rather mean character. To prevent the need for ever greater demands on imagination, let me assure you that until you told us a few minutes ago, I had not the slightest idea Dora had either capital to leave or that she intended to leave it to me.' He waited, then said: 'You don't believe that?'

'I have no concrete reason to believe or disbelieve you at present.'

'So you'll content yourself with merely surmising I murdered Dora?'

'Stop it!' Laura said furiously.

'Right. We call a moratorium on supposition, suspicion, and susceptive possibility, and have another drink.'

'Señor, unfortunately there is one more question I have to ask.'

'Then get it over with.'

'Where were you last Tuesday evening?'

'Which is when Dora died?'

There was no answer.

'You are asking for my alibi?'

'That is so.'

'Charles was here all the time,' Laura said fiercely.

'Would it be possible to corroborate that fact?' Alvarez asked.

'Haven't I just done so?'

'Someone other than yourself, Señora.'

'You are calling me a liar?'

'I would not do so.'

'Because you're too mealy-mouthed to come out with it?'

'Because I always believe a person until I have reason not to.'

Gerrard said: 'Then since Laura's telling the truth, I have an alibi.' He stood. 'If you'll pass me your glass, Inspector?'

'I don't think the Inspector has time for another drink,' Laura said.

Alvarez admired the courteous way in which she had told him to bugger off. A Mallorquin could also show good manners.

He stood. 'Thank you for your help, Señora, and for your hospitality.'

She ignored him.

He walked through the house. As he opened the front door, Gerrard hurried up. 'I'm sorry about that.'

'There is nothing to apologise for, Señor.'

'Laura is very protective.'

'Of course.'

'She found it very difficult to understand that you are obliged to suspect me.'

'It is my unfortunate duty, however unlikely it seems.'

As Alvarez drove away, his thoughts were confused. Had Gerrard's facetious, courteous manner suggested guilt or innocence? If innocence, wouldn't he have protested that innocence with more vigour? A Mallorquin would have been shouting. If he was guilty, would he have introduced the possibility of guilt instead of waiting for his accuser to do so? Had innocence been arming him or had his manner been a cloak for guilt?

Fourteen

The phone awoke Alvarez. He dragged himself upright, reached across the desk, and lifted the receiver.

'Were you fast asleep?' Salas demanded.

'At this time of the day, Señor?'

'Then why did it take you all afternoon to answer?'

'I was downstairs, checking some evidence, and had just started to climb the stairs when I heard the phone in my room ring. I came up as quickly as I could.'

'Then you should start taking exercise ... Have you established whether the Englishwoman drowned accidentally or was murdered?'

'Not yet, Señor. It is a confusing case.'

'Which it was bound to become in your hands. Have you made any progress at all?'

'In a negative way, yes.'

'Do I have to point out that progress should be made in a positive way?'

'I have raised certain questions which have

to be answered.'

'It has not yet occurred to you to answer them?'

'I judged it best to continue the investigation in reverse.'

'A decision that you no doubt found quite logical.'

'That was because of something you said. Rather, that you didn't say.'

'Alvarez, have you a family history of mental deficiency?'

'Not as far as I know.'

'Then your knowledge probably does not extend far enough since you believe a case should be conducted in a negative, reverse manner because of something your superior chief did not say.'

'I have been told there was an Irishman who held that when one wants to hear the truth one should listen to what is not said.'

'Then we may take it there is Irish blood in you. Have you conducted any inquiries which can be considered even faintly constructive?'

'As you said, Señor, motive is very often the key to the case. So identify a strong motive for the Señorita's death and it becomes much more likely she was murdered rather than that she drowned accidentally.'

'Have you established a motive?'

'Señor Gerrard is Lady Gerrard's brother-in-law. While she is clearly a very wealthy woman, he is equally obviously very far from wealthy since he and his wife live in a caseta. I don't know of any other foreigners who are in such reduced circumstances as they...'

'I should prefer not to listen to all you don't know since I want to return home before midnight.'

'Lady Gerrard owns the caseta and until now, Señor Gerrard has paid no rent, but she is demanding he starts to do so. Again, the trust – which manages the estate belonging to Lady Gerrard; at least, as far as I can understand the position, that is...'

'Do not try to explain and confuse matters inextricably.'

'Dale, Señor Gerrard's son, is at public school in England. The fees are very considerable and although the trust has been paying them, Lady Gerrard has said it will no longer do so. Señor Gerrard cannot afford to pay these, so...'

'Why is the financial situation of these foreigners of the slightest consequence?'

'I was coming to that.'

'Then do so more succinctly.'

'Dora Coates possessed a bungalow which is valued at a hundred and twenty thousand pounds and she had over eighty thousand pounds in two banks...'

'How do you know that?'

'I've received a fax from England.'

'When?'

'Recently, Señor, and this is the first opportunity I've had to report it to you. The details the fax provided may well prove very relevant.'

'In what way?'

'Señor Gerrard is the main beneficiary under Señorita Coates's will. He stands to inherit everything but a thousand pounds and some furniture.'

'Have you questioned him?'

'He denies having had any knowledge of the will or the contents.'

'You find it likely he would do otherwise? I don't suppose it occurred to you to ask if he could supply an alibi covering the relevant times?'

'Indeed, I did. His wife confirms they were at home and neither of them left the house that night.'

'There is no independent confirmation?'

'No.'

'Have you made inquiries in Port Llueso to determine whether he was seen down there during the relevant period?'

'Not yet.'

'Why not?'

'There's hardly been time...'

'A mantra for inefficiency. Is there any further evidence to suggest his guilt?'

'None. And despite the obvious motive, I find it difficult to believe he would ever commit murder.'

'On what grounds?'

'He is an English gentleman.'

'You like to judge guilt on character, not facts? ... And clearly you need to be reminded that they were English "gentlemen" who were the pirates who plundered our treasure galleons as they returned from the New World.'

'That's a long time ago.'

'National character does not change.'

'Which in a way is what I was saying...'

'Have you found the time to question Short? Or do you consider him also to be a gentleman?'

'He's far from one. And, of course, he was not only in the port at the relevant time, by his own account, he waded into the sea.'

'But being facts, such details are of small account?'

'From the beginning, he has been the obvious suspect. But there is no apparent motive for his having murdered his aunt; indeed, you could say he had a negative motive for not doing so.'

'I should prefer not to.'

'All he inherits on her death is a thousand pounds and the contents of her house and these seem to be almost valueless. Since she paid for his holiday, it must be reasonable to assume she might well have offered him further benefits, so her death presents him with a potential loss.'

'Gerrard is the only suspect?'

'Yes. But as I said earlier...'

'Then there is no need to repeat yourself.'

'But wouldn't you agree with me...'

'Only ever reluctantly.'

'...that accidental drowning has become more likely than murder?'

'Until you can be certain no one saw Señor Gerrard in Port Llueso that Tuesday night, that the incision on the victim's head was not caused by a fingernail, that the cry which was heard was not a cry of terror, that you have failed to identify further possible motives for murder, that an English gentleman is incapable of acting now as he has so often in the past, I should not make the egregious mistake of offering a judgement.' He cut the connection.

Alvarez checked the time, was irritated to learn he would have to wait before he returned home for a well-earned rest or the question might be asked, why hadn't he driven down to the port and begun inquiries to ascertain whether Gerrard had been seen there on the Tuesday evening. Only a man of Salas's intemperate character would suggest so thankless a task. What were the odds against success?

The phone rang. He stared at it with fresh annoyance. The rush of life had deprived man of the benefits of ignorance. Before modern means of communication, a problem could not instantly be passed on and so there was always a very good chance it would have been sorted out one way or the other by the time an inspector in the Cuerpo was informed about it. He finally lifted the receiver.

'You've got...' The sound faded.

It returned. '... here quick.'

'What's the problem?'

'I just told you.'

'I couldn't hear most of what you were saying.'

'The mobile don't work well here and there ain't no telephone even though Telefonica promised...' Once again, the sound faded. It returned. 'The body what Marta found is in one of the fields back of the olives.'

'Where are you speaking from?'

'Vall d'en Fangat.'

The valley was in the mountains, at least three-quarters of an hour's drive away. 'Call the Guardia and tell them there's a body to collect.'

'It's them what told me to tell you.'

There were always some who would go to any lengths to avoid their duty. 'Get back on to them and...'

'They can't do nothing because it's murder.'

'How can they know it is?'

'Because I told 'em.'

'You are an expert criminologist?'

'I don't reckon a man bashes in his own head. But maybe you know different?'

'He's probably a foreigner who was stupid enough to go rock climbing and fell.'

'When the field's in the middle of the valley?'

'Where exactly are you talking from?' Alvarez asked angrily.

The mobile signal faded twice before the answer was clear enough to be understood. 'Ca Na Echa.'

'Whereabouts in the valley is that?'

'At the end.'

'It would be.'

'How's that?'

'I'll be along as soon as I can make it.' He cut the connection, dialled Palma.

'Yes?' said the plum-voiced secretary.

'It's Inspector Alvarez. I need to speak to the superior chief.'

'He's not here. What do you want?'

'I have to report a serious incident.'

'Would it not be an idea to report it, then?'

It was small wonder she had never married. 'I have just been informed that the body of a man has been found in a field in Vall d'en Fangat and wounds to his head suggest a second party was involved in his death.'

'His identity?'

'Unknown at the moment.'

'I will inform the superior chief as soon as possible.'

He sighed as he replaced the receiver. His problem no longer was how long he must wait before he returned home; now it was, how long was it going to be before he returned home?

Fifteen

The valley ran north to south, cutting into the Serra de Tramuntana, which ran west to east the length of the island; in sharp contrast to the often dramatically weather-sculptured bare rock sides, the bottom was level and the land good enough to grow fig, olive, and almond trees and, where there was irrigation, vegetables and some of the sweetest melons on the island. In the past, the few families had lived there in what had been virtual isolation because it was accepted that after puberty, the women could cast the evil eye on beast or human. Everyone knew the story of Julia Caimari. She had left the valley to visit the village of Mesquida and there had had an argument with the owner of a small shop; two days later, the owner had died suddenly and in great pain. Six men from Mesquida, one of whom had been the owner's cousin, had courageously entered the valley, caught Julia, bound her, and thrown her down the deepest well.

When in the course of time each of the six died, relatives blamed his death on the witch's curse.

It was odd, Alvarez reflected as he drove into the valley, how short a time it was since there had been people so ignorantly superstitious ... He passed a woman who was irrigating several rows of sweet peppers and carefully smiled at her.

Ca Na Echa was a typical, unreformed Mallorquin farmhouse. Oblong, walls of stone, roof tiles laid on bamboo, windows small, it offered shelter, but little comfort; family lived on the top floor, animals on the ground one.

As he braked to a halt in front of a rusting wire trellis over which an extensive vine grew, a man came out of the house, stopped, and silently watched him climb out of the car. 'Are you Bautista?' he asked as he shut the car door.

'Who wants to know?'

'I do.'

'Who are you?'

'Inspector Alvarez of the Cuerpo.'

'Was it you what I spoke to?'

'Why d'you think I'm here?'

'How do I know why you're here?'

Most would have been annoyed by this apparent stupidity, but Alvarez was not;

185

stupidity had for centuries been almost the only defence a peasant had against authority. 'Who found the body?'

'Marta.'

'Is she your wife?'

'Think I've a bit on the side?'

'You both live here?'

'In the village.'

'So who does live here?'

'Ain't no one.'

'But it is your property?'

'Why d'you think I'm here?' Bautista replied, relishing the chance to repeat Alvarez's words.

Times changed, even in a 'forgotten' valley. Only a few years before, Bautista and his wife would have lived in Ca Na Echa, accepting discomfort and lack of any amenities as their lot in life. But circumstances, and particularly television, had encouraged them not to remain content and when they had had the chance – probably one of them had inherited a village property – they had quickly moved to enjoy a modern life. Now, they worked the land, but left the house empty. Sooner or later, a foreigner, seeking dramatic beauty and solitude, would offer them so high a price for the property, they would be unable to refuse it, even though a peasant valued land almost beyond gold.

The new owner would have electricity brought into the valley, the house would be reformed and its character lost, his friends would envy him his life amidst this rustic idyll and in consequence would buy and reform other houses, and before long the memory of Julia Caimari would be forgotten.

'Maybe you ain't nothing better to do but stand there, but I have,' Bautista said.

'First, you can show me the body.'

Bautista led the way down the dirt track to the road where he turned right, to face the end of the valley and a thousand-metre mountain whose lower slopes were covered with pine trees. His pace was such that Alvarez was soon sweating. 'Why didn't you say it was so far away? We should have come in the car.'

'Ain't fit, is you?' Bautista answered with scorn.

'Fit enough.'

'For sitting on your arse?'

Alvarez was convinced Bautista was walking more quickly than he would normally have done in order to humiliate him.

They stopped at a field in which were irregularly spaced olive trees whose gnarled, twisted short trunks and relatively long branches spoke of past pruning, but recent neglect; around those on the right, there was thick garriga – the typical island brush, a mixture of plants which included grass, brambles, wild lavender, rosemary, thyme, gladioli, irises, rock roses, and a very occasional orchid.

'By that tree.' Bautista pointed to an olive, a hundred metres in from the road.

Alvarez walked across. An objectionable smell, at first slight, became very much stronger before the body of a man initially became only partially visible because of the masking effect of the garriga in which it lay. Visually examining the ground before each step, he stopped half a metre from the body. The man, probably in his late twenties, was dressed in a T-shirt on which was printed in English, 'Let's see if we fit', jeans, and trainers. He had dark, curly black hair and a noticeably broad nose; his wide mouth was partially open, his eyes closed, and his lips were tensed as if a call for help had been begun, cut short and 'frozen'; he had either been trying to grow a beard or favoured long stubble; his right cheek was stained with blood. Amongst the hair on the crown of his head was a scalp wound in which a small section of shattered skull was visible.

The garriga was undisturbed except in the immediate area of the body, so a struggle seemed unlikely; there must have been considerable bleeding, but there was no blood on the vegetation. Almost certainly, Alvarez judged, the body had been dumped there in the hope that if ever found, this would not be before the forces of decay made it unidentifiable.

'Do you know him?' he asked.

'No,' Bautista replied.

'What brought your wife over here?'

'What d' you mean?'

'It's not a corner of the field to which anyone normally comes, judging by the look of the vegetation, so I wondered why she did?'

'She was searching for a lamb.'

'You run sheep here?'

'Ain't you got eyes?' Bautista pointed up at the lower slopes of the nearest mountain.

Alvarez studied the rising, rock-strewn land and finally identified several sheep, their colour making them not readily visible against the background. 'I'll need to talk to your wife. Is she back at the house?'

'Picking the vegetables for the market tomorrow.'

After finding a body, a townswoman would probably be too shocked to do anything useful; for a peasant, violent death was little more traumatic than the violence of birth. 'I'll want to use your mobile.'

'Why?'

'To call the police doctor to certify death.'

'If you can't see he's dead, you're a useless sort of detective.'

'There'll be those who agree with that.'

Bautista was annoyed that he had failed to anger Alvarez.

'Where is your mobile?'

'Why ain't you got one?'

'The Cuerpo doesn't provide it.'

'Then it ain't up to me to do their job for them.'

'That's fair enough. So I'll drive to the village and make the call from there. Of course, you'll have to wait until I return and everything's sorted out; I hope that won't be too long after it's dark.'

Bautista muttered angrily before he led the way out of the field and along the road, now walking so quickly that Alvarez no longer tried to keep up; better to be humiliated than to suffer a heart attack.

Marta was by the base of the outside stone steps up to the top floor of Ca Na Echa. Small, thin, her face darkened and leathered by sun, wind, and rain, she looked several years older than her husband, but was a year younger.

'D'you show him?' she asked, her voice deep and throaty.

'Yes,' Bautista replied.

'What's he say?'

'Don't know if the man's dead.'

'Is he blind?'

'Likely.'

Alvarez asserted his presence. 'I have to call the doctor to examine the body, not to confirm death, but to give an opinion on the circumstances of it, so I need to use your mobile.'

She said nothing.

'Your husband said it's in the house.'

'Maybe.'

'Upstairs?'

'Unless you reckon we keep it with the animals.'

He waited for one of them to move, but neither did. He climbed the steeply pitched stairs – more quickly than he would have done had neither of them been watching – and opened a battered door to enter a square room with bamboo and tile ceiling and bare concrete floor. A large aspidistra in a heavily worked copper bowl stood in the centre and the only furniture was a square wooden table and three arm-chairs which had had a hard life. On one wall hung two large framed photographs of parents or grandparents, taken many years before. The man wore a wide-brimmed hat, white shirt without a collar, black waistcoat and short coat, voluminous plus-fours, socks and shoes; the woman, a blouse, a long-sleeved sweater with a neckband of intricate crochet work, and a high-waisted, very long skirt. He appeared embarrassed, she stared directly at the camera with a look which made one wonder if she had possessed ... The mobile was on the table. He picked it up, returned outside and stopped on the top step. 'What's the pin number?' he called out.

The Bautistas looked uneasily at each other.

They were afraid to give him the number for fear he would use it to his advantage and their disadvantage. He made his way down the steps, handed the mobile to Bautista. 'Put it in.'

When the mobile was handed back to him, he dialled the post, spoke to a cabo and asked him to send the police doctor, photographer, and undertaker to Ca Na Echa. He handed the mobile back and Bautista switched it off.

'Shall we go inside for a chat?'

For a while neither of them moved, then as if to an unspoken command, they made for the stairs. Alvarez followed at a more leisurely pace, but was breathless when he sat on the only unoccupied chair.

He took a handkerchief from his trouser pocket and mopped his forehead. 'It's unusually hot for May.'

'Not for them what ain't as fat as a matana pig,' Bautista said.

Rather than cause further resentment, he said lightly: 'Fat or thin, it's thirsty weather.'

'You want a drink? There's water down in the well.'

A humorist, he thought sourly. He spoke to Marta. 'Tell me exactly what happened.'

'I found him,' she answered.

'What about before you found him?'

'I didn't know he was there.'

Was she mocking him under the guise of peasant stupidity? He wasn't certain. There were limits to his sympathetic understanding and when he next spoke, his voice was much sharper. 'I need to know why you went into the field, what you did before you saw the body, what you did then and afterwards. And I'm afraid you're going to have to stay here until I do.'

She spoke in a toneless voice as she stared at the concrete floor. The sheep were free to roam the field and the lower slopes of the mountain. Each day, either she or her husband looked them over to make certain they weren't becoming flyblown or suffering from foot rot, or had injured themselves on one of the rocks which littered the land. The previous day, she'd noticed one of the lambs had seemed hunchy, so she'd kept a special eye out for it – failing to see it, she'd crossed towards the far corner of the field because animals went there for the shade. She'd smelled death and, believing the lamb had succumbed, had gone forward expecting to find its corpse ... Instead, there had been the dead man.

'How close to him did you go?'

After considerable thought, she said: 'Two metres, maybe.'

'Then you didn't touch him?'

'You think I'm daft?'

'When was the last time you were in that part of the field?'

She looked at her husband, shrugged her shoulders.

'Yesterday, the day before?'

'Ain't no need to go there when there ain't nothing missing.'

'So it could be several days?'

She did not respond.

Alvarez looked at his watch. It was almost seven. The doctor, photographer, and undertaker would be at least another fifteen to twenty minutes before they arrived and there was no judging how long they would take. He was not going to be home in time for a drink before supper, perhaps not even for supper. He could be certain that somewhere about the building would be many bottles of homemade wine which might taste more of earth than the mountain dew beloved of wine critics, but would be far preferable to the water he would be offered if he again remarked what thirsty weather it was ... Abstinence made the imagination run faster. Perhaps Dolores had bought a bottle of Imperial as an unexpected present and even now was preparing Entrecote amb albercocs to accompany it...

The doctor straightened up. 'I can't add much that isn't obvious.' He was a tall, thin man with a round face that would have better suited a short, fat man. 'He was hit probably more than once on the head with something heavy and must have lost consciousness, if not died, immediately. No other signs of injury are visible. Time of death is as imprecise as ever, but the absence of rigor and the slight degree of decomposition suggest a couple of days ago. The lack of lividity in parts of the body which were in contact with the earth suggests he did not die where found, but was left there after death; this would seem to be confirmed by the absence of any blood on the ground or the vegetation. As you'll know, it's surprisingly difficult for one person to move a dead body of any size and weight and so either more than one person or some form of carrying instrument is usually necessary; there is a strand of coloured wool stuck to his T-shirt by dried blood, which might have come from whatever he was carried in. I can't tell you any more than that.'

Photographs having been taken, the body was removed in a bodybag. As the undertaker's van drove away, Alvarez crossed to his parked car and opened the driving door.

There was a shout from Bautista. 'You owe for the call on me mobile.'

'Send the bill to the superior chief in Palma.' Alvarez settled behind the wheel and slammed the door shut. Would Dolores have been in a good mood and put his meal in the oven to keep warm?

Sixteen

As Alvarez entered the post somewhat later than usual, the duty cabo looked up from the newspaper he had been reading. 'Someone's been shouting for you.'

'Who?'

'How would I know?'

'By asking.'

'Wasn't me took the call.'

Feckless, Alvarez thought as he crossed to the stairs and climbed them. In his room, he settled in the chair and noted with pleasure there was no post. He closed his eyes, the better to decide on his priorities for the day...

The phone awoke him. Teresa Jiminez spoke with such nervous haste that at times it was only with difficulty he understood her. Her son, Francisco, had not been to see her for many days...

'You would have expected him to?'

Francisco was a wonderful son, the best a mother ever bore; he visited or phoned her almost every day to make certain she was well. Yet she had not seen or heard from him for days.

'Have you spoken to any of his friends to ask if they know where he is and if he's all right?'

She'd spoken to Jacobo Beltrán who was like a brother, but he knew nothing. She was certain something terrible had happened to her beloved son...

He tried to calm her fears by saying that most youngsters who went missing turned up within the first few days. 'Where does he live?'

'He shares a place with Jacobo. I have said to him, many times, why pay a fortune in rent when there is a bedroom here that costs nothing...'

'What's the address?'

'Casa Jasumella, in Carrer Talaia, which is in the port...'

'I know the road. Does Francisco have a job?'

As if he would be a layabout! Both he and Jacobo worked for Carlos, the builder. She'd begged him to find another job because building was so dangerous – Cousin Jorge had fallen to his death when scaffolding collapsed because no one had made certain it had been properly erected. And everyone knew what kind of a man Carlos was. He built houses for the foreigners and always smiled to make them think he was a good man, but he charged them far more than he should. Of course, all foreigners were so foolish, they allowed themselves to be swindled...

'Describe Francisco,' he said, hoping she would picture a man with straight brown hair who always shaved each morning. Her description closely matched that of the dead man found in Le Vall d'en Fangat. 'I'll make inquiries right away.'

Once again, she expressed her fears. Alvarez tactfully brought the conversation to an end, replaced the receiver, and stared unseeingly through the unshuttered window at the sun-washed wall of the building on the other side of the road. Of all the jobs a policeman had to do, imparting tragic news was the worst.

It took forty-five minutes to learn where the small firm of builders were working, another twenty to drive to the site in the centre of the flat land between Llueso and the bay. A metre-high rush fence had been erected on top of the rock wall which bordered the road, an indication that permission had not been granted to build.

He opened the gates and drove in; as he stopped, a barrel-shaped man, stripped to the waist, spotted with sandstone dust, came out of the half-built house and up to the car. 'You want something?' he demanded through the opened window, his belligerence tinged with uneasiness.

'Cuerpo. Is Francisco Jiminez here?'

'Ain't been from Monday on.'

'Then I'll have a word with Jacobo Beltrán.'

'About what?'

'That's between him and me.'

'I ain't having him off work, so you can come back when we knock off for grub.'

'And leave me with nothing to do but wonder whether the ayuntamiento knows you're building here?'

'You lot don't give a man a chance to make an honest living.'

'Which maybe is why so many of you make dishonest ones.'

Carlos muttered something, turned and went back into the house; a couple of minutes later, Beltrán – tall, handsome in an oily manner – came across to the Ibiza. 'What's up, then?' he asked.

Alvarez stepped out of the car. 'I've had a call from Francisco's mother and she's very worried because she hasn't heard from him in days.'

'You're here because of him?'

'Yes.'

Beltrán became aggressively self-confident. 'She fusses over him like an old hen.'

'Does that mean you have seen him very recently?'

'No, it don't.'

'But you're not concerned?'

'Not really.'

'Why not?'

'I guess it's just he's found the courage to get shacked up.'

'And forgot to contact his mother or come to work?'

He sniggered. 'It's always good the first time.'

'Do you know what woman he's with?'

'Can't say since I wasn't with him when he clicked.'

'Then you've no idea where he might be?'

'That's right.'

'His mother told me you and he share a place in the port. Is there likely to be a photograph of him there?'

'Could be, I suppose.'

'Then get in the car.'

'Here, I ain't done nothing wrong.'

'Nothing I know about. You're going with me to look for a photograph of him.'

'I don't understand.'

'No one's asking you to. Get in the car.'

They reached the port seventeen minutes later. Carrer Talaia had once been the boundary of the seaside village and beyond it had been green fields, a few cultivated, most too stony to grow anything but trees, now it was surrounded by blocks of flats; once, Casa Jasumella had been a fisherman's cottage, now it was owned by a Mallorquin widow who let it for a rent that would have astonished her late husband.

Beltrán led the way into the front room. 'Haven't had time to tidy up,' he muttered.

Alvarez looked at the empty beer bottles, dirty glasses, plates, and cutlery, the shirt and socks thrown onto one of the worn-out chairs, and wondered if the time was ever found. 'See if you can find a photo of him.'

Beltrán went through the far doorway. Alvarez, avoiding a plate on the floor, crossed to the low glass-topped table – the glass was cracked – and picked up one of the soft-porn magazines on it. Unimaginative. The second, no better, had been covering a brochure for the BMW Z4. For those with a love of cars, but not the money to buy their choices, the brochure could be as frustrating as the magazines.

Beltrán returned and handed Alvarez a

photograph. In this, he was in swimming trunks and in close embrace with a lissom woman in a monokini; by their side stood a second man, his head turned so that much of his face was in shadow. The shape of the head, that part of the face which was visible, the build of the body, made Alvarez reasonably certain the murdered man in Le Vall d'en Fangat was Francisco Jiminez, but he needed a more definite identification before bringing tragedy into the mother's life. 'I think Francisco is dead.'

'Jesus!'

'But I can't be certain, so you have to come to the morgue to make a positive identification.'

'No way.'

'It has to be done.'

'Not by me, it doesn't.'

'By you.'

'Why not his mother?'

'Because there's one chance in a hundred the dead man is not Francisco,' Alvarez replied contemptuously.

'Look, I just can't do something like that.'

'You'll find you can.'

Beltrán went over to the table and picked up one of the dirty glasses, left the room; when he returned, the glass was filled with red wine. 'Can't you get someone else?'

'No.'

He drank.

'Who took the photograph?'

'The other woman,' Beltrán answered, before he slumped down on one of the chairs, to the accompanying twang of springs.

'How long ago was it taken?'

'How do I know?'

'By remembering.'

'You don't understand, I can't look at a body...'

'When was the photograph taken?'

Beltrán drank. 'Maybe earlier this month.'

'Who was the other woman?'

'I don't know.'

'I want a name.'

'I can't remember what it was.'

'Think harder.'

In a rush of words, Beltrán tried to explain. He liked the ladies and they liked him so most warm evenings he'd walk the beach and chat to likely prospects; since there was always one willing to enjoy a spot of fun, it was impossible to remember who was who.

'If you...' Alvarez checked what he had been about to say. The woman's identity was unlikely to be relevant, so why pursue the question? Because she would be attractive and almost certainly enjoyed a spot of fun, so should he meet and question her...? There was no greater traitor than one's own mind.

Beltrán interrupted his thoughts. 'Are you sure it's him?'

'No. Which is why you're coming to the morgue.'

Beltrán drained his glass, hurried out of the room to refill it. For once, Alvarez had not remarked on the thirsty weather – there were still places where one could buy fifty-cent wine. When Beltrán returned, fear and alcohol prompted his tongue. Where women were concerned, Francisco was odd. Not that odd, just odd. Liked to talk about them, to buy magazines and videos, but face to face was scared of them. He, Beltrán, always had to make the contact for both of them and usually Francisco made such a cock-up of chatting up his companion, he returned to the house on his own. And there had been the time when a sound had made him think Francisco was spying on him and his woman – he'd not made certain because one couldn't leap off the bed in the middle, could one? Then there were the night-vision binoculars. Francisco had said he'd bought them to study wild animals at night. That was a laugh!

'You're suggesting Francisco's fun was

peeping?'

'I reckon.'

'So if he is the victim, it's very unlikely he ran into trouble because he was playing around with someone else's woman, it was because he was peeping.'

'You're saying ... You're saying he was murdered?'

'Yes.'

Beltrán drank the wine in the glass, stood. 'I need another.'

'Better take it easy if you don't want to feel queasy even before we reach the morgue,' Alvarez said uncharitably.

Seventeen

In the office, Alvarez thought up several reasons for not phoning Salas, but regretfully decided none of them would sound convincing if challenged. He dialled Palma and after the customary wait was put through to the superior chief. 'Señor, yesterday, some time after we had spoken over the phone, I was informed that a body had been found in Le Vall d'en Fangat and injuries to the head suggested murder. I spoke to your secretary and told her...'

'That you knew virtually nothing. If you have further information, why am I only receiving it now?'

'Señor, I arrived at the office very early in order to make my report to you, but there was a phone call from Teresa Jiminez to say she feared her son was missing. Since there had to be the possibility he was the murdered man, I decided it was necessary to check whether that was so before reporting to you, knowing how you like all the facts...'

'There is no need to repeat yourself.'

'I asked her to describe her son and what she told me made me reasonably certain the dead man was he. I could, of course, at this point have phoned you, but since the identity of the dead man was so important, I decided first to speak to Jacobo Beltrán, who shared a small house in Port Llueso with Francisco Jiminez. He showed me a photograph of Jiminez. This seemed to confirm the identification while still leaving room for doubt, so I have arranged to drive Beltrán to the morgue this afternoon.'

'What was the doctor's opinion?'

'That the dead man had probably been struck more than once on the head with a heavy object. He was fairly certain the victim had not died where he was found and possibly had been carried there, bundled up in some form of woollen material.'

'Who is Francisco Jiminez?'

'He's from Port Llueso and works for a builder. It's possible he is, or was, not quite normal.'

'Physically or mentally abnormal?'

'I suppose one would call it mentally.'

'From what form of mental instability did he suffer?'

'He didn't get on with women.'

'You suppose that to be abnormal?'

'He enjoyed pornography, but was shy meeting them and didn't...' He became silent.

'Well? Didn't what?'

'You know.'

'If I knew, I should not ask.'

'Didn't get cracking.'

'I have had to learn that on this island there is not the level of intelligent communication one expects in Madrid, but you manage to reduce almost any conversation to incomprehensibility. What was he supposed to crack?'

'He didn't try to seduce the woman he was with.'

'Even though your past attitude should have forewarned me, I am surprised and disheartened you should obviously regard such reticence as abnormal rather than the behaviour of an upright man.'

In a moment of pure mental aberration, Alvarez said, 'Perhaps his problem was the lack of uprightness.'

'What's that?'

'Nothing, Señor.'

'I find it abhorrent that you seek to introduce sex into every case.'

'If it's there...'

'Only the impure delight in seeking out impurity.'

'But I think it's important to know what kind of sex life Jiminez led.'

'I am not surprised. However, to someone of a balanced mind, that will be a matter of neither importance nor interest.'

'Not if it identifies the motive for his murder? He was probably sexually immature – perhaps because of an over-protective mother...'

'You will leave such supposition to those psychologists who are content to spend grubby professional lives.'

'Because of his immaturity, he gained his kicks from peeping.'

'And therefore, because of your predilections, this case is affording you considerable interest?'

'Beltrán reckons Jiminez used to try to peep on him when he was with a woman in the bedroom and they...'

'You will refrain from lascivious supposition.'

'Another thing. He'd bought himself a pair of night-vision binoculars.'

'That is of significance?'

'It meant he could go out at night and watch couples who believed the dark hid what they were doing.'

'Listening to you is like visiting Sodom and Gomorrah.'

'It seems possible he was caught peeping on a couple and the man was so furious, he hit Jiminez over the head, killing him. He panicked, removed the body in a rug, and tried to hide it where he thought it wouldn't be found until decayed beyond the likelihood of ever being positively identified. Of course, if that is what happened, it must prove very difficult to identify him; doubly difficult if he's a foreigner who might well have already left the island.'

'You seek excuses for failure already?'

'Señor, I'm just pointing out that with thousands of possible suspects, unless the post-mortem can provide a definite pointer to the murderer's identity...'

'One must hope the p.m. provides not only a definite pointer, but one that gives you no further opportunity to pursue interests that a cultivated man will eschew.' He cut the connection.

Alvarez replaced the receiver. Had the superior chief always been as obnoxious? The phone rang. He lifted the receiver. 'Inspector Alvarez...'

'Unfortunately, I am only too aware of who – I am tempted to add, what – you are,' said Salas. 'Have you considered the possibility there is a link between the murder of Jiminez, if that's who the dead man is, and

Señorita Coates?'

'Yes, Señor, and in my opinion there can be none.'

He rang off.

It was still very early to leave for home, yet Salas was unlikely to phone again and the thought of a drink before lunch – Bacalao con pasas y huevos duros? – outweighed any sense of caution.

The assistant slid out the refrigerated compartment, one of twelve, to its full length. Beltrán was sweating heavily and he kept plucking at the neck of his shirt as if it was too tight, rather than unbuttoned and open. The assistant pulled back the green sheet to reveal the dead man's head, not yet repaired and cleaned as it would be before burial.

'Is it Francisco?' Alvarez asked.

Beltrán swallowed heavily; he nodded.

'You're quite certain?'

He began to retch.

'Through there, turn right,' said the assistant as he pointed. He watched Beltrán rush through the doorway. 'Hope he makes it or there'll be more work for me.' He pushed the compartment back into the unit.

'Is the professor here?' Alvarez asked.

'Can't rightly say. Best ask upstairs.'

He made his way to the office of Professor

Fortunato; a secretary told him the professor was away at a conference, but Mateo Sastre, who had conducted the post-mortem, would be able to speak to him.

Sastre could provide little information of immediate consequence. Jiminez had been killed by two blows, perhaps three, from a heavy instrument; a piece of bark embedded in the skull suggested a section of branch rather than anything metallic; the bark, quite fresh, had already been identified as coming from an almond tree.

There was no reason to doubt the doctor's assessment that death had occurred two to three days before the body was found. Green and purple staining had begun to spread from the...

Alvarez tried not to listen.

The doctor had been correct that the presence and absence of lividity, still faintly visible, showed the victim had not been killed in the position in which his body had been found. Very probably, it had been bundled into something – a blanket or rug, judging by the single woollen thread on the clothing – and transported to the field where it was dumped.

There was nothing else to report.

Alvarez made his way downstairs and along to the 'Communing' room, a place of peaceful colours, comfortable chairs, fresh flowers, religious tracts, and supposedly soothing piped music. Beltrán had regained some composure.

'If you're ready, we'll leave,' Alvarez said.

'I feel terrible.'

'A coñac will set you up.'

He led the way out on to the street and along to a small café which had four tables set out on the pavement. They sat; almost immediately, a man came out and took their order.

'Who could have done it?' Beltrán asked, his voice shaky.

'I'm hoping you'll help me answer that.'

'You think I know? I swear I didn't have anything to do with it...'

'I'm sure you didn't,' Alvarez answered confidently – murderers came in many shapes and sizes, but none of them Beltrán's. 'But perhaps you'll be able to tell me something that will enable me to identify who did. For the moment, I'm assuming Francisco was out peeping, was caught by a man who was so furious he grabbed a length of wood and struck him. So to your knowledge, did Francisco go out peeping at the weekend?'

'I don't know.'

'Think back.'

'I can't.'

It seemed the questioning would have to wait. The waiter returned with two brandies. Beltrán drank his as if it were medicine, Alvarez almost as quickly, but with pleasure. As he placed the empty glass down on the table, he thought about ordering another but remembered Traffic was proposing to set up road-blocks in certain areas and to breathalyse every driver. A wasteful exercise, since the quality of the driving of any Mallorquin was equally poor whether drunk or sober.

By prior arrangement, Beltrán was in Casa Jasumella when Alvarez arrived on Thursday morning. No attempt had been made to clean the sitting-room and on one of the plates a piece of food was beginning to grow fungus.

'Carlos is going to create hell with me for not being at work again,' Beltrán complained.

'Tell him to come and complain to me.'

He hesitated, then said: 'Do you want a drink?'

'No, thanks,' Alvarez answered.

'You don't mind if I do?'

'Why should I, so long as you remain reasonably coherent.'

Beltrán hurried out of the room, returned with a glass of red wine. He sat. 'I don't know anything...'

'I won't know what you do know until I find out what you don't.'

As he looked uneasily at Alvarez, his hand shook sufficiently to cause ripples in the wine.

'Think back to the weekend and tell me whether Francisco went out Saturday, Sunday, and Monday nights.'

After a long drink, Beltrán said: 'Didn't go out Saturday. Bit odd that.'

'Why?'

'He usually went off because there were more people around.'

'What about Sunday night?'

'He was out then.'

'And Monday?'

'He wasn't here.'

'Not even in the morning?'

'That's right.'

'So when was the last time you saw him on Sunday?'

'After me and the blonde had come back. She asked why Francisco was alone and I said he was shy, so she said, why didn't he join in our fun? I told him what she suggested – he hardly spoke English – but he said he had to go out. Came over all nervous, more like.'

'What time would that have been?'

'Maybe ten.'

'So he was going out to peep?'

'I don't reckon he was.'

'Why not?'

'He never took his binoculars.'

'How can you be so certain if you were busy?'

'They're still in his room, that's how.'

'Show me.'

Beltrán drained his glass, stood, led the way through to a small bedroom; the bed was unmade, clothes were strewn over a chair, several pornographic magazines were on the floor, two drawers in the built-in cupboard were open, their contents in chaos. He pointed at the battered bamboo table on which was a leather case.

Alvarez opened the case, brought out the strangely shaped binoculars. Had Jiminez just been escaping a situation which embarrassed him? If peeping was his pleasure, after such an invitation why hadn't he welcomed the chance to stay, even if he lacked the courage to take part? ... Then he had met someone and had been murdered, probably not because he had been peeping – confirmed by the fact he had been battered to death with a branch of an almond

217

tree, something unlikely to be found on a beach, his natural peeping ground. Yet if peeping had not been the motive for his murder, what had? ... Memory supplied a possible answer.

'I can't tell you no more,' Beltrán said, worried by Alvarez's continuing silence.

'When I was last here, I saw a brochure for a BMW Z4. Are you thinking of buying one?'

'You think I'm as daft as Francisco? It's him brought the brochure back from Palma.'

'Did he reckon he'd buy one?'

'Wanted to know what I thought was the best colour, which engine to have, where could he keep it when there's no garage and if it was parked in the street some kid might run a coin along the paintwork.'

'If he was serious, he must have been highly paid.'

'Him? All he was good for was lumping things around. Get him to lay a line of tiles and it ended up a zig-zag.'

'Then how was he going to pay for a car like that?'

'He wasn't, was he? He talked more balls than a politician.'

'Had he recently been spending a great deal of money?'

'Wasn't easy to get him to meet the rent after he'd paid up on the bank loan he needed to buy the binoculars.'

'Did you notice any other signs of his seeming to think he'd have plenty of money in the future?'

'Yeah, but like I said, he was full of talk. Me and him would go on a cruise and meet some wonderful birds – wouldn't have done him much good! He'd buy a villa and we'd live like foreigners.'

'Did he explain where the money would come from?'

'I asked him once when I was totally freaked out with all his talk, and he just grinned his stupid grin ... Ain't going to grin no more. Can't stop thinking about him in the morgue...' He stood, picked up his glass and left the room.

With bitter annoyance, Alvarez realised he should have remembered that the only real certainty in this world was uncertainty. It seemed he would have to tell Salas that there was after all the possibility of a connection between Dora Coates's death and Jiminez's.

Eighteen

Laura opened the front door of Ca'n Dento. 'Good evening, Inspector.'

'I'm afraid I have some more questions to ask, Señora.'

'Then you'd better come in.'

As he stepped inside, he was once more aware of how attractive she was, an attraction which had much less to do with physical appearance than warmth of character.

'We're outside, enjoying sundowners. I hope you'll join us?'

'As we say, "The man who refuses a copa is tired of life." '

She led the way through to the small, vine-covered patio. Gerrard stood. 'A pleasure to see you again.'

'You're very kind to say that, Señor.'

'More insurance than kindness.'

'Charles,' she said, 'just for once, curb the humour.'

'Like a good husband, to hear is to obey ... Sit down, Inspector, and tell me what I can get you to drink?'

'May I have a coñac, with just ice,' Alvarez answered as he sat.

'I'll bring out some more crisps.' Gerrard picked up an empty earthenware bowl, went indoors.

'Have you...?' Laura began, then stopped.

'Have I discovered the circumstances in which Señorita Coates died? No, Señora, I'm afraid I have not.'

'Then you're here because you still think ... You must understand. Charles couldn't ever do anything so terrible as commit murder, however desperately hard up he was. And he really had no idea Dora would leave him anything.' She was silent for a few seconds, then said, her tone now despondent: 'But, of course, you'd expect me to say all that.'

'Not with such conviction.'

'That ... that's a strange thing to say.' She turned her head to stare straight at him. 'Are you silently laughing at me?'

'Why should I do such a thing?'

'Because I probably sounded incredibly naive.'

'I think the truth is often naive.'

'Do you?'

'Does the Inspector what?' Gerrard asked, as he returned to the patio, a tray in his hand.

'Think truth is often naive.'

He put the tray on the table, straightened up. 'Not a line of conversation often heard in social chit-chat. What prompted the question?'

'I was telling the Inspector you would never hurt Dora and you'd no idea she would leave you anything in her will.'

'Regretfully, the Inspector probably will not turn his views around and accept naivety often is truth.'

'One day...'

'One day, I'll learn the value of silence?' he said. He passed a glass to her and one to Alvarez, sat. 'You wouldn't be here, Inspector, unless you still thought I might in some way be implicated.'

'Proving a negative can be as important as proving a positive, Señor.'

'What negative are you seeking to prove?'

'That you were not in Port Llueso on Tuesday evening, the twentieth.'

'I'm not trying to be smart, but aren't you slightly mixed up? Your goal surely is to prove I was down there.'

'Were that so, it would not be a negative.'

'You realise you're in danger of suggesting you don't believe I had anything to do with her death?'

'That I hope you didn't.'

Gerrard drank. 'An odd thing for a detective to say to a suspect.'

'The truth is often odd as well as naive. When I last spoke to you, I asked if you could provide corroborative evidence to prove you were at home all that evening, but you were unable to do so. Since then, have you remembered anything which might help to do so?'

'We were here, on our own.'

'No one phoned before or after eleven o'clock?'

Gerrard looked at Laura.

'I don't remember anyone calling us,' she said.

'You didn't phone anyone?'

'I don't think so. I wish to God I could say one of us had, but it wouldn't be the truth.'

'Señor, I must ask you for a photograph of yourself.'

'Why?'

'I will show this to people in the port to find out if they can remember seeing you that night.'

'When the port's full of people whose memories of night-times are often poor since some of the bars still have happy hours, I'd have thought searching for the proverbial needle in a haystack would be likely to be more productive. And if no one claims to have seen me, that's no better than an unproven negative.'

'It is my superior who demands I do this, despite the problems.'

'And like most Señors, problems are for solving by others?'

Alvarez briefly smiled. 'There is another matter which has to be considered. Did you know Francisco Jiminez?'

'No.'

'His body was found on Tuesday; he had been murdered.'

'You're surely to God not now thinking Charles also had anything to do with his death?' Laura said, her voice high.

'Señora, as I have said before, I have to consider all possibilities, however improbable they seem ... Señor, do you know Le Vall d'en Fangat?'

'I don't have any idea where it is.'

'Then you didn't drive to the valley last Sunday?'

'No.'

'Where were you Sunday night?'

'Here.'

'No, we weren't,' she said. 'We had the royal invitation.'

'So we did! Dinner with my sister-in-law. I had forgotten. The meal was excellent because Ana is a queen among cooks –

although Heloise can do nothing but criticise her – the ambience somewhat different, a fact which, since you know quite a lot about our relations with our relation, will not surprise you.'

'She asked us because she wanted to enjoy the pleasure of reminding us we still hadn't paid the first tranche of rent and the satisfaction of providing a meal which she knew we could not have afforded,' Laura said.

'I wonder if she's really capable of such subtlety?' Gerrard said.

'Because you mistake the form for the substance.'

'When did you leave her house?' Alvarez asked.

'Frankly, I've no idea what the time was when Laura said we should leave because I had become too talkative. The blame for which lies squarely on the Vega Sicilia.'

'On you for drinking most of the bottle,' Laura said.

'What is a man to do when he is repeatedly offered nectar by a butler who understands the male priorities?'

'Depends if he has any self-control ... You asked what the time was, Inspector. We were home by half eleven.'

'What did you do then?'

'Went to bed, of course.'

Alvarez spoke to Gerrard. 'You did not drive anywhere?'

'Inspector,' she said, 'if he had set off to drive to the village, he would not have arrived.'

Alvarez drained his glass. 'Thank you for your help.'

'That was the last question?' Gerrard asked.

'Yes, Señor.'

'Then before I get the refills, you can answer one question from me. What makes you believe it possible I could have murdered a man I have never met?'

'Perhaps I am again intent on deciding you could not.'

'Another negative?' He waited, but when Alvarez said nothing, stood, collected the tray and three empty glasses, went into the house.

He must remember to ask for the photograph, Alvarez told himself.

He parked in front of Ca'n Jerome, crossed to the portico, rang the bell. Filipe opened the door. 'Is the Señora in?' he asked.

'Regrettably.'

He followed Filipe through the house and out to the swimming pool. Heloise, wearing a bikini, was lying on a patio chaise longue, the lower half of her body in sunshine, the upper half in the shade of the sun umbrella set in the centre of a small circular table; on the table was an ice bucket in which was a bottle of Veuve Clicquot, an empty glass, and a plate on which were several small squares of smoked salmon and brown bread.

She berated Filipe for again not finding out whether or not she was at home before introducing a visitor, then faced Alvarez. 'What do you want this time?'

'A word with you, Señora,' Alvarez answered.

'Lady Gerrard,' she sharply corrected. 'None of you seems to have any memory whatsoever. I am not going to have my evening interrupted, so if you must, you can come back some other time.'

'I am making inquiries into a murder.'

'So you've said often enough. And I've answered all your ridiculous questions.'

'This does not concern the death of Señora Coates, but of Francisco Jiminez.'

'I've never heard of him. Filipe, show this man out.'

'I not think that good,' Filipe said uneasily.

'You are not paid to give opinions.'

'Lady Gerrard, if you will answer my questions...' Alvarez began.

'I have no intention of doing so.'

'Then I must arrange for you to be brought down to the post so that I can question you there.'

'Are you daring to threaten me?'

'I am explaining the alternative to speaking to me now.'

'You are quite incapable of understanding I will not be treated like some suburban housewife.'

'I would speak to anyone else as I am speaking to you.'

'I don't doubt that, since you lack any manners and all respect.'

'We have a saying, "The duke and the pot-boy breathe the same air".'

'You will be much more conversant with the air the pot-boy breathes. Well, why are you still standing there?'

'To learn whether you prefer to answer my questions here or at the post.'

'I suppose one must make allowances for ignorance.' She spoke sharply to Filipe. 'Haven't you any work to do?'

Filipe left.

'What is it you want to know?' she snapped.

Alvarez moved a patio chair and sat.

'Make yourself at home, won't you?'

'Thank you, Lady Gerrard.'

Her anger increased, but his blank expression convinced her he lacked any social nous and so had not realised her words had been sarcastic. She lifted the bottle out of the ice bucket and filled her glass.

'Is it correct Señor and Señora Gerrard came here to supper on Sunday?' he asked.

'It is not.'

'They told me they were invited here.'

'To dinner, not supper.'

'Then did they come to dinner on Sunday?'

She drank. 'That is none of your concern.'

'May I remind you I am conducting an investigation into the murder of Francisco Jiminez.'

'Your unwelcome presence makes any reminder unnecessary. And it is an insult to suggest I could have any connection whatsoever with this man.'

'Whether you did or did not is something I have to determine.'

'Are you now daring to accuse me of murder? I've had enough of this. Tomorrow morning, I'll complain about how appallingly I have been insulted.'

'I do not think it is insulting for a member of the Cuerpo to ask questions of someone who may be able to help in an important investigation.'

'In England, the police have sufficient common sense not to imagine someone like me could begin to know anything.'

'This is Spain.'

She picked up a square of bread and salmon, ate. 'Your uncouth manners,' she said through her mouthful, 'make it all too obvious this is Spain, not England.'

'Did Señor and Señora Gerrard have dinner with you on Sunday night?'

She emptied her glass, refilled it, drank. 'Yes,' she finally answered.

'When did they leave here?'

'Some good while after they should have done.'

'If you would give me a time?'

'It wasn't until well after eleven. My brother-in-law drank far too much and I finally had to make it clear I considered they should leave.'

'Would you describe him as being drunk?'

'Not to you.'

A sudden and unusual sense of family loyalty or a refusal to share such information with the likes of him? As he thanked her for her help, she picked up another square of bread and smoked salmon, ate.

He left.

Nineteen

Alvarez drove slowly as he marshalled his thoughts in order to be able to present the facts clearly and concisely to Salas. He parked under the shade of a palm tree, left the car, and walked along the narrow street, constantly forced to move to one side or the other by the stream of advancing pedestrians. Such was the present rush of life, it was difficult to remember when the road had been unsurfaced and had known the clop of mules and the creak of carts, old women had set chairs outside their houses and gossiped, knife-grinder, bottle-buyer, fishmonger, or umbrella-mender had announced his presence with conch shell, bell, or shout, and had worked or sold in the street. But when one did recall such times, one also remembered there had been many who could not afford to eat wholesome food, send children to school, consult the doctor when ill, or die with dignity...

He entered the post, passed the desk at

which the duty cabo should have been sitting, climbed the stairs, entered his room, switched on the fan, slumped down in the chair, and used a handkerchief to mop the sweat from his neck and forehead. Before the tourists' invasion, there had been little crime and that quickly dealt with because poor roads, lack of transport, and shared poverty made for isolated and enclosed communities in which everyone knew everyone else's business; an inspector in the Cuerpo was not stressed all day, every day, trying to solve the insoluble...

When he awoke, he phoned Palma.

'Well?' said Salas.

'I have to report on my investigations into the murder of Francisco Jiminez...'

'What devil's mess of things have you made now?'

'Señor, nothing has gone wrong.'

'You expect me to believe that when you make a report on your own initiative?'

'I have questioned Jacobo Beltrán and...'

'Who are you talking about?'

'He was a friend of Jiminez and they shared a house in the port.'

'You expect me to know that without being told?'

'I did report this to you...'

'I have little sympathy for an officer who

232

uses imagination to try to cover up his incompetence.'

'But I can distinctly remember telling you...'

'Did you learn anything of relevance from this Beltrán?'

'Jiminez left the house Sunday evening. He did not return that night and was not there or at work on Monday. Whilst this is obviously only circumstantial evidence that he died late on Sunday night or early Monday morning, remembering the forensic evidence, I think we can accept that that is the period of time.' He waited for a comment, continued when there was none. 'When he left the house on Sunday evening, he did not take his binoculars with him.'

'Why is that of any significance?'

'Had he intended to go peeping – it was his custom...'

'There is no call for you to indulge yourself.'

'But previously, it had seemed most probable he was murdered because he had peeped on a couple who were...'

'You did not understand what I have just said?'

'I think it's necessary to put forward the proposition in order to deny it.'

'In your hands, logic gains fresh meaning.'

'Señor, that he did not take his binoculars must mean he was not intending to peep and was not killed by an enraged man who caught him. His murder was planned, a fact borne out by the knowledge he was battered to death with a piece of branch from an almond tree – the possibility of finding that by chance when suddenly needing a weapon is surely too slim to consider? Again, a sudden and unplanned murder must normally leave a man so shocked, he cannot collect his thoughts; the murderer was sufficiently clear-headed to remove the body from where it had fallen and carry it to the field in Le Vall d'en Fangat where he believed there was sufficient undergrowth for it to remain undiscovered until it had become unidentifiable – his mistake was not to know that where sheep are kept, someone will be looking after them.

'Jiminez was an ordinary man...'

'You consider a man with perverted habits to be normal?'

'Ordinary, in the sense that to the outside world he lived a normal, run-of-the-mill life. So who could have a motive, unconnected with his peeping, for murdering him?

'When I was in his house, questioning Beltrán, I saw a brochure for a BMW Z4. Of course, many people collect brochures of expensive things they cannot hope to own, but I asked Beltrán if Jiminez had intended to buy such a car. He told me Jiminez had absurdly been talking about doing so.

'I decided to contact the BMW agents on the island and I spoke to a salesman and asked him if he remembered talking to a customer whose description I gave. The salesman recalled such man who had talked about buying a BMW Z4 and had asked endless questions about optional extras, but as it had seemed unlikely he was someone who could afford that expensive a car, the salesman had viewed him as more of a nuisance than a prospective buyer.

'Coupling peeping with this apparent belief he would soon be wealthy – he had also talked about going on an expensive cruise and buying a villa – and the possibility of blackmail is raised. Perhaps he had seen someone doing something who, he believed, would pay him large sums of money to remain quiet.

'What act could be so heinous it had to be kept hidden even at the cost of murder? It was unlikely to be of a sexual nature...'

'Why?'

'Where adults are concerned, these days there are no boundaries and it is impossible to name an act that would arouse such odium it had to be concealed, no matter what.'

'What you find impossible, most would, regrettably, find only too possible.'

'Señor, I think Jiminez saw through his night-vision binoculars the death of Señor-ita Coates. Someone was holding her head under water.'

'Did you not assure me, very recently, there could be no connection between the deaths of the two victims?'

'I did not then have the information I do now.'

'And you did not understand it is unwise to deliver an opinion before all the facts are known?'

'I have always thought crime detection calls for possibilities to be suggested, which are then confirmed, denied, or adjusted, as more information is gathered. Pursuing an incorrect theory can often lead to the evidence which supports the corrected one, a kind of negative positive; or would you say, a positive negative?'

'As a very busy man, I should not waste my time with either. Can you name the murderer?'

'If I'm right, it's someone who had a motive for killing Señorita Coates.'

'Your ability to state the obvious cannot be

challenged. Who had that motive other than Gerrard and Short?'

'As I have mentioned before, it was to Señor Short's advantage that Señorita Coates lived.'

'And to Señor Gerrard's that she died. Is there not yet sufficient evidence to arrest him?'

'No, Señor.'

'Because it would call for effort to uncover it? Have you questioned him about his movements on Sunday night?'

'He and his wife had supper with ... That is, dinner.'

'What are you talking about?'

'I understand the English have dinner, not supper, in the evening.'

'Then when do they have supper?'

'I don't know.'

'It would be helpful, if very limiting, if you only introduced subjects about which you know at least something.'

'He and his wife ate an evening meal with Lady Gerrard. He drank rather heavily, but since he was served Vega Sicilia that is hardly surprising...'

'On this island, an immoderate consumption of alcohol is never surprising. Was he drunk?'

'His wife described him as incapable of

driving.'

'Since he would need to drive a car to carry a body to the valley, one would expect her to say that.'

'Yes. But...'

'Well?'

'I just can't see him committing one murder, let alone two.'

'He faced exposure as the murderer of Señorita Coates – you do not consider that fact provides the strongest motive?'

'I'm sure he's the kind of man who would suffer anything rather than deliberately hurt a woman; if innocent of her death, he had no motive for killing Jiminez.'

'Your judgement of character is, no doubt, on a par with your ability to conduct a case according to the rules. Have you yet questioned people in the port to find out if someone saw him down there on the night Señorita Coates died?'

Intention could be as good as the deed. 'Indeed, Señor. I obtained a photograph of him and am showing this to people likely to remember him, such as waiters in cafés and restaurants; without any success. I'm afraid the chances of success are so small that might it not be better if I spent my time...'

'You will continue until you find someone who did see him.' Salas cut the connection.

Diego Bonet watched Alvarez cross the foyer of Hotel Monterray and when within earshot, said: 'You'll be giving us a bad name.'

'Is Señor Short around?'

He turned and visually checked the key board. 'He's not up in his room so I guess he's on the beach with his woman.'

'Is she still the one with big tits?'

'Funny how that's the first thing a certain type of person notices.'

'If you don't understand why, I'm sorry for you. So is she?'

'Yes.'

Minutes later, Alvarez found Short amongst the sunbathers. He lay on his back on a towel and by his side was the blonde, once again topless.

Short raised himself up on his elbows. 'Not again!'

'What's the matter now?' she asked.

'How the hell would I know?'

'Can't he understand how you feel and that he makes things much worse when he keeps on reminding you?' she asked.

'You think he gives a damn how I feel?'

She sat up and stared at Alvarez. 'Don't you have any consideration for other people's feelings?'

239

She was not wearing sun glasses and her eyes were coloured the deep blue of the waters of the bay; her moist, full lips were shaped for love; her breasts, now shaped by gravity ... Alvarez reined in his thoughts. 'Señorita, had I not a duty to carry out, I would not disturb either of you at such a time, but I have to speak to the Señor.'

'If you...'

'Leave it, Gemmy,' Short said. He stood. 'If anyone turns up while I'm gone and suggests a trip on his yacht, tell him you suffer from seasickness.' He leaned over and kissed her, then straightened up and, ignoring Alvarez, walked to the hotel.

Alvarez spoke to Diego. 'Is the office free?'

'I'll check.' He looked into the office, turned back. 'It's all yours.'

As Short sat on the chair in front of the desk, he said: 'So what's it this time? You think I didn't do my best to stop her from going swimming when it was dark and she was tight; that I didn't do my damnedest to find her in time; that I don't wish over and over again I'd had one less drink at the hotel bar because then I might have found her because she hadn't drifted so far?'

'I am not here to ask you about the sad death of your aunt.'

'What then?'

There was a knock on the door and a waiter entered; he handed Alvarez a glass, asked Short if he would like a drink, and having been told not, left.

'Have you hired a car whilst you've been here?' Alvarez asked.

'What the hell is this? What's it matter if I have?'

'Just answer the question.'

'And if the answer's yes?'

'Where is it?'

'At the back of the hotel.'

'It will have to be taken away to be examined.'

'What's bugging you? Little green men from Mars?'

'Have you been driving around the island?'

'Would I hire a car to park it here all the time?'

'Have you been to Le Vall d'en Fangat?'

'Not as far as I know. But I can't remember the names of half the places I've seen.'

'Then you might have gone there without realising it?'

'Could have gone anywhere.'

'The body of a man has been found in the valley. He was murdered.'

'Not born lucky.'

'You are unconcerned?'

241

'Look, I'm not going to worry about someone I didn't know when I'm still mourning my aunt.'

'Did you know Francisco Jiminez?'

'No.'

Alvarez drank. 'Where were you on Sunday?'

'Here.'

'In the evening?'

'Morning, afternoon, evening.'

'Can anyone vouch for that?'

'Gemma.'

'Your friend on the beach?'

'If she is still on the beach.'

'You were together all evening until you went to bed?'

'Yes.'

'When did you go to bed?'

'Could have been any time; it was when she said she was tired.'

'You didn't leave the hotel again until the morning?'

'No.'

'You didn't drive anywhere that night?'

'Like I've bloody well said over and over. And this was meant to be a holiday!'

Alvarez stood. 'You can show me where your car is parked so I can tell Vehicles, who will be collecting it.'

'Without any say-so from me?'

'It will be returned as soon as possible.' And since there wasn't the shadow of a motive, the search would be a waste of time and effort. However, Alvarez thought as he finished the brandy, at least it would be somebody else's time and effort.

Escobar lived in one of the new apartment blocks at the back of the port. A lift took Alvarez up to the third floor and a short walk along the passage to flat 3D. A woman in her late twenties, her face expressing great tiredness, her full belly and a screaming child the cause of this, said her husband had just woken and she'd tell him to come along to the sitting-room.

As Alvarez waited, he looked through the north-facing window at the mountains. In the sharp sunshine, they possessed the beauty of natural behemoths and were seemingly clothed in peace. Yet many years ago, men who favoured the wrong ideology had been taken up into them to be shot. Beauty could hide ugliness as easily as justice, injustice.

Escobar, bleary-eyed, entered the room and slumped down on one of the chairs as his wife asked if they'd like coffee, then left to make it. A three-year-old child rushed in, saw Alvarez and came to an abrupt stop, hesitated, then went over to her father and in a scramble of words complained that her mother wouldn't let her eat any more chocolate. He tried to explain that too much chocolate was bad for little girls; certain he was not going to help her, she began to cry and shout until her mother hurriedly appeared and swept her out of the room.

'Have you any kids?' Escobar asked wearily.

'None I know about.'

'If she woke me up once since I got back from the hotel today, it was half a dozen times. They say kids cement a marriage. Bloody Mallorquin cement for my money.'

'I'm very sorry to have to bother you like this, but it really is necessary. I'll be as quick as possible. When did you go on duty on Sunday night?'

'Twenty hundred hours, as always.'

'Do you remember seeing Colin Short that evening?'

'Sunday was when María's cousin turned up to cause more trouble.' He thought for a while. 'Remember the girlfriend more than him, if you know what I mean. She was wearing a frock that made one wonder if it would stay up. He was with her.'

'You saw him at what sort of time?'

'They were going up to their rooms –

more likely room.'

'Can you be more definite?'

'I'd say it was between ten and eleven.'

'Did you see him again?'

'No.'

'You're certain he didn't leave the hotel later on?'

'As certain as I can be.'

'Is there a way of leaving without going through the foyer?'

'Sure, but it's staff only.'

'Is there anything to stop a guest using that exit?'

'Not if he knows about it.'

'Where is it?'

'At the back – leads on to Carrer Balmes.'

'That's it, then. You can go back to sleep.'

'With a kid creating hell?'

Twenty

Alvarez stared at the top of the desk. He had learned nothing to alter the facts. If Dora Coates had not drowned accidentally, the only known motive for her murder implicated Gerrard; yet if character was as strong an indicator of a man's actions as he believed it to be, Gerrard would never murder. Since the investigation had uncovered no further motive for her death, then despite the evidence of the incision on her head and the sand under her nails, the drowning was probably accidental. Accept that and there could be no connection between her death and Jiminez's and he must change his opinion once again.

How to make his next report without its seemingly pointing to incompetence on his part? Since Salas invariably chose to believe the worst, surely that was by definition, impossible. So all he could do was square his shoulders ... But did an intelligent man jump off a cliff in order to reach its base? He carefully climbed down. So how to assure Salas he was pursuing further, promising leads, in the hopes that, by spreading out time, something would turn up which would enable him to appear in a better light?

Sometimes, inspiration needed a shove. He opened the bottom right-hand drawer, brought out bottle and glass, poured himself a brandy. Inspiration failed to strike by the time the glass was empty, so he poured a second drink. And it was when this was half gone that he remembered the money in Dora Coates's hotel bedroom. It had been strange she should have so much in cash and so little in travellers' cheques – common sense said it should have been the other way round. Although elderly people did odd things, there was no proof that she had been motivated by senility, so surely it could be made to seem reasonable to try to confirm the source of the cash, since one of the basic tenets of good crime investigation was to identify and concentrate on the unusual. England could be asked to confirm Dora Coates had drawn the euros from her bank. Requests from other countries were always given low priority and it would be days, perhaps weeks, before there was a response. And in order to show he was not content to wait to hear from England, but with eager initiative was determined to pursue every possibility, he would get on to the local banks and ask if any of them, between the times of her arrival on the island and her death, had paid out over two thousand euros in cash to a customer.

He had a third drink as a gesture of self-congratulation. One could ring a field with a two-metre-high fence, but a clever lamb would always find a way over or under it.

Since there was no time like the present (for later convincing the superior chief he was always on the button), he spoke over the phone to Fortega, who worked in one of the local bank branches, a man he knew well after years of trying convincingly to promise he would soon clear his indebted account. 'I want to know if anyone, perhaps a foreigner, has recently withdrawn over two thousand euros in cash. Could one draw that much with plastic?'

'Not from our ATM, certainly, and probably not from anyone else's. We're not geared up to billionaires with black cards.'

'Would you like to ring me when you know the answer?'

'No need for that. Hang on.'

Alvarez was annoyed to be left waiting, phone to his ear.

'I just had to confirm what I remembered.

One customer, a foreigner, demanded two thousand five hundred euros in cash. It stuck in my mind because not only was the amount unusually high for a private withdrawal, we were short and had to get notes from our other branch in the village.'

Alvarez silently swore. He had expected this line of inquiry to take days, yet ironically his first call brought a result. 'Who drew the money?'

'That's customer confidential.'

'And I'm a customer.'

'Lady Gerrard.'

'Who?' Surprise caused him to shout.

'You near broke my ear drum.' He repeated the name.

'Well, I'll be damned!'

'Has she been up to something she shouldn't?'

'I hope so.'

'You've obviously met her! Call her a bitch and you're insulting female dogs. One day she came in and demanded...'

Alvarez listened without understanding what was being said, his mind in too much chaos. Had he been asked to name the most unlikely person to give a starving waif a crust of bread, he would have named Heloise Gerrard, yet it seemed possible she had given Dora Coates two thousand five hundred euros. Or was it a coincidence; had she drawn the money for her own selfish use? Or had Dora brought the money found in her handbag from England? Or had Dora been given that by someone else?

'Is there anything more you want to know?'

'A basketful, but you won't be able to tell me.'

After he'd thanked the other and rung off, Alvarez poured himself a fourth drink. He wasn't certain whether it was a congratulatory or commiserative one.

Filipe opened the front door. 'You've chosen a bad day if you've come to talk to her.'

'Why's that?' Alvarez asked, as he stepped inside.

'There was a phone call earlier on and since then she's been making everyone's life hell.'

'Have you any idea what the call was about?'

'You think I listen in to her conversations?'

'If you have the chance.'

'I couldn't understand all she said because she was keeping her voice down, but it was to do with money. She wanted more and it sounded as if whoever she was speaking to wasn't going to give her any. Funny thing about the rich – they're never content.'

'That's because there's always someone richer. Where is she?'

'In the library. But this time, I'd better tell her you're here.'

Filipe left, returned within the minute. 'She won't see you.'

'She's no choice.'

'You can explain that.'

'Then show me the way.'

They went into the sitting-room and through a doorway to a corridor, along that to the library at the end. Heloise sat at a pedestal desk; when she saw Alvarez, anger lined her face. 'What does this mean?' she demanded.

'I have to speak to you, Lady Gerrard.'

'Were you not told I would not receive you?'

'Nevertheless...'

'Nevertheless, you have forced your way into my presence.'

'Hardly forced.'

'Leave immediately or I'll call the police.'

'I am the police ... I should like to ask you if you have recently drawn a large sum in cash from a bank?'

'That is none of your business.'

'I am afraid it has become so. I can assure you that what you tell me...'

'I will tell you nothing and I regard any assurance from you as worthless.'

'I'm sorry you should think so. What bank did you use?'

'You are unable to understand plain English? Whether I have drawn any money from my bank is none of your concern and so I have no intention of answering your question.'

'I have been informed two thousand five hundred euros in cash were recently withdrawn by you.'

'How dare you grub into my affairs.'

'Why did you need so large a sum in cash?'

'This is monstrous!'

'Was it to pay Señorita Dora Coates?'

She stared at him, her expression now one of shock rather than anger.

'Was it?'

She stood, pushing her chair back with unnecessary force as she did so.

'Why do you find it difficult to answer?'

She turned away and he could no longer see her full face; in profile, years and character became more obvious.

She spoke in a taut voice. 'I will explain, merely to ensure you cease bothering me and leave. In England, people from a certain background acknowledge that privilege brings responsibility – a concept unknown in this place. When one has employed a servant who has retired, one recognises an obligation to concern oneself with her welfare. So when Dora Coates was here, showing the eagerness, common to her class, to impart details of her personal affairs, she told me how long she had had to save in order to come out to the island with her nephew. Since it became clear she could have virtually nothing to spend whilst here, I gave her a small sum to enable her to have a happier holiday, hoping she wouldn't waste it on the usual tourist trash.'

'I should not call two thousand five hundred euros a small amount.'

'I am not surprised.'

'In fact, Señorita Coates was hardly a poor woman. At her death, she owned property and a considerable sum in the bank, thanks to an employer who had named her in his will. As she was so ready to speak about herself to you, I am surprised she did not mention her good fortune.'

She stood, crossed to a bell-push on the wall, pressed it. As she returned to her chair, Filipe entered. 'The Inspector is leaving,' she said.

Alvarez led the way out of the room. At the front door, he said: 'You told me she was annoyed when Señorita Coates and her nephew came here to see her?'

'Bloody furious.'

'Yet she's just said she gave Señorita Coates a very handsome present because it's the custom in England to be concerned with the welfare of past employees.'

'You think she'll give a shit about Ana and me after we leave here?'

Alvarez stepped outside and crossed to his car.

He was enjoying his second cup of hot chocolate and second ensaimada of the morning when the phone rang.

Dolores, who was chopping up white onions, said: 'Is it ridiculous for me to think you might answer that since I am so busy?'

'It's Saturday.'

'Which leaves you even less capable than on the other six days of the week?'

'I'm certain the call won't be for me.'

She dropped the knife she had been using, tore off a sheet of kitchen roll, and wiped her fingers. 'The more trouble a man believes he can save himself, the more certain he becomes.' She hurried out of the kitchen.

He pulled off a piece of ensaimada and dipped it in the hot chocolate. Women could be very small-minded; they refused to understand that when men worked very hard all week while they did nothing but potter around the house, the men were entitled to rest over the weekend.

She returned to the kitchen. 'So it couldn't be for you!' She picked up the knife and resumed chopping with greater force. 'As my mother used to say, "Ask a Madrileño the time and he'll criticise you for not owning a watch." '

'What are you on about?'

'Your superior chief demands to speak to you.'

'Impossible!'

'Then you can tell the speaker he is every bit as rude as the man he is imitating.'

'But it's Saturday.'

'Even were it a Sunday, such a man would never discover any manners.'

'Why's he phoning me at the weekend?'

'Perhaps if you speak to him, he will tell you.'

Alvarez made his way through to the front room, picked up the receiver. 'Good morning, Señor.'

'Why the devil aren't you at the post?'

He looked across at the small carriage clock above the fireplace and was surprised to note the time was nearly ten. 'Because of the pressures, Señor, I was at work very early. One of my tasks was to question a man who, I hoped, would be able to help me in one of my investigations. Unfortunately, he proved unable to do so. As I had not had breakfast, due to my very early start, I thought it reasonable to return home briefly to have something to eat ... Are you ringing because something is wrong, Señor?'

'You are so inept as to be unable to appreciate the appalling trouble you have caused?'

'What am I supposed to have done to cause anyone any trouble?'

'You force you way into the home of a noble English lady; you insult her; you inform her that without her knowledge you have been investigating her bank accounts; you imply she is a liar; yet it doesn't occur to you she might find such action unwelcome?'

'I did not force my way into Ca'n Jerome, I was shown in by the butler.'

'Who informed you, you were not welcome.'

'I had to speak to the Señora. I was very careful not to insult her.'

'She is of a very different opinion.'

'Then it's her opinion against mine.'

'Leaving no difficulty in deciding whose to accept.'

'I did make enquiries as to whether she

had withdrawn a large amount of cash from her bank.'

'With her permission?'

'Since I had not actual proof to rely on, I thought it must be more tactful to...'

'Tact is not a word you should feel free to use.'

'I did not imply she was a liar.'

'She did not tell you Señorita Coates was not well off and you did not say you were surprised the Señorita had not mentioned her good fortune?'

There was a brief silence.

'Well? You find it difficult to answer?'

'Yes, Señor. There are so many negatives I'm not certain what is the question.'

'In the past, you have all too often shown your unsuitability for the position you hold; by calling a noble English lady a liar, by secretly investigating her financial affairs and thereby suggesting she might be engaged in an illegal enterprise, you have proved your unsuitability for any position. I am making a full report of the matter to the director-general, to which I shall attach my recommendation as to what action should be taken. In the meantime, and until his decision is made, you will continue working, but on no account will you have further contact with Lady Gerrard. Is that clear?'

'But I believe she should be questioned further. I think she may hold the key to solving the deaths of Señorita Coates and...'

'Have you been able to identify a motive for the Señorita's death other than Señor Gerrard's?'

'Not yet. But I am certain he did not kill her.'

'A conclusion based on your expert knowledge of human psychology?'

'During a case, one can get a feeling that...'

'Efficient officers prefer facts to feelings. And only by entering the fantasies of a person with perverse interests can one suppose Lady Gerrard knows anything about the murder of Jiminez. Perhaps you are about to suggest she wielded the branch which smashed his head?' Salas slammed down the receiver.

Alvarez returned to the dining-room, where he brought a bottle out of the sideboard; he continued through to the kitchen. As he poured brandy, he expected to hear harsh words about men who dug early graves for themselves, but Dolores said, her voice filled with sympathy: 'He was even more obnoxious than usual?'

He nodded.

Twenty-One

Would Heloise, who by her treatment of her brother-in-law had exposed her mean, vindictive nature, have given Dora Coates two thousand five hundred euros merely in order to enjoy a financially carefree holiday? Alvarez wondered, as he sat in the office. Even if there were those in England who still defied modern attitudes and taxes and honoured noblesse oblige, she surely was not one of them. She considered no one but herself. Then why had she paid this sum to Dora Coates, whose previous visits had so annoyed her? Blackmail was one answer, but was it a feasible one? Had Dora been murdered to prevent further blackmail? Had Jiminez observed her murder through his binoculars and decided to blackmail the blackmailer, not understanding the danger this could entail?

Blackmail concerning what? Sex had once been a constant probability, but in the past decades all restraints had disappeared so that now it was very difficult to suggest an activity, the threat of the exposure of which would be sufficient to provoke murder. Money? If one enjoyed the benefits of a large trust, one did not need to defraud or steal ... Then perhaps his judgement of character was as poor as Salas believed; perhaps Lady Gerrard proved that one person could at different times possess opposite characteristics – be honest or dishonest, kind or cruel, generous or mean, depending on circumstances. If so, then she might well have freely given Dora Coates that money.

He was a fool to keep asking himself unanswerable questions; more especially when he had been forbidden to question Lady Gerrard again.

The phone rang. Vehicles in Palma reported that they had completed their search of the Renault Mégane, hired by Colin Short, and there was nothing to report.

'Are you sure there's not a single trace?' Alvarez asked.

'You'd like to come here and spend a few hours trying to prove us wrong?'

'It's just I thought that...'

'Then best think again.'

It was still relatively early, but he needed cheering up. He left the office and went to

Club Llueso for his merienda. When, three-quarters of an hour later, he returned, the phone was ringing.

'The superior chief wishes to speak to you,' said the plum-voiced secretary in her haughtiest tones.

'Where the devil have you been?' Salas demanded. 'I've been trying to get in touch with you for the past half-hour.'

'Señor, I have been...'

'Questioning someone who lives near your home? ... I have spoken to the director-general and he accepts my recommendations. You are to appear before the hearing which will be convened to decide whether, in view of your incompetent and insolent behaviour, you are a fit person to remain in the Cuerpo. Until the hearing, a relief inspector will be detailed to the Llueso area; you will work with him, offering such assistance as you are capable of giving.'

'Señor, I am convinced...'

Salas rang off.

Misfortune seldom walked alone. Of all his fellow inspectors, Alvarez disliked Rios the most. Rios made a point of dressing smartly, deferring to superiors, and enjoying work. As if that were not enough to damn him, he was a committed teetotaller.

He arrived in the middle of Tuesday morning and announced he was taking charge from that moment.

'I gathered it was more a case of our working together,' Alvarez objected.

'You gathered incorrectly. I am to take charge of all investigations and you are to assist me ... should I require you to do so,' he ended curtly.

Alvarez silently accepted that, in the eyes of Rios, he had done himself no favours by forgetting to shave that morning and not changing his shirt, which had become slightly stained during breakfast.

'To begin with, I need your projections for all the investigations in hand.'

'Projections?'

'Notes on each case, with particular reference to facts established and facts still to be determined, plus the proposed course of inquiries.'

'I don't work quite like that.'

'Even though that is the course laid down in the Manual of Procedure?'

'Is it?'

Rios crossed to the opened window and looked out. 'I begin to understand why the superior chief said what he did.'

'Which was what?'

'It was a confidential discussion.' He

turned back. 'I naturally will be concentrating on the two major crimes, the deaths of Señorita Coates and Jiminez. I understand you have made little or no progress in either case.'

'That's not strictly so.'

'Have you, then, determined whether the Señorita drowned accidentally or was murdered?'

'I'm convinced she was either murdered or allowed to drown when she could easily have been saved.'

'Successful investigation calls for certainty. From what the superior chief has told me, it is essential to question Señor Gerrard far more energetically and expertly than you have done since he had an obvious, indeed, the only, motive for her death.'

'Maybe, but one can't ignore character...'

'One should pursue the obvious in preference to the arcane. I understand you have made no more progress in investigating the murder of Jiminez than the death of Señorita Coates?'

'I'm certain I've established the motive for his killing. He was a peeper...'

'The superior chief mentioned that unhealthy interests were liable to surface in your work.'

'Jiminez observed Señorita Coates's death

and he either then or later identified the man who had pressed her head under the water or had been standing when he should have been saving. Later he tried to blackmail that person, never realising the danger of this.'

'What is the proof?'

'As yet, there is none.'

'It is pure supposition?'

'Which is based on facts.'

'The interpretation of which is a skilled task so it will be necessary for me to study your notes. When you've handed me those, you can for the moment work on whatever other and minor cases are in hand, reporting regularly to me.'

There was a silence.

'The notes.'

'There aren't any.'

Rios spoke as if he had just been informed that a pterodactyl was advancing on him. 'You've been conducting two major investigations and haven't a single written note pertaining to either?'

'I can tell you all the known facts.'

'I am not surprised it has been indicated I might be assigned to this area on a permanent basis.'

It seemed, Alvarez thought miserably, the official hearing into his conduct had reached its verdict even before being convened.

Dolores looked across the table. 'Are you feeling ill?' she asked Alvarez. When he did not answer immediately, she said: 'Are you in pain?'

'I'm all right.'

'Then why are you not eating what has taken me all morning, slaving in the kitchen, to prepare?'

'I'm not hungry.'

'I know why,' Juan said. 'Uncle's chasing after a woman who's so much younger, she runs rings around him.'

'How dare you!' Dolores said angrily.

'That's what you said the other day when...'

'Another word and you'll go up to your room and stay there until tea time.'

'But you did...'

'You did not understand what I have just said?'

Juan tried to kick Isabel under the table because she had been silently jeering at him.

Alvarez refilled his glass.

'If you're ever going to catch one, she'll have to be older than you or you never will catch up!' Jaime sniggered until Dolores looked at him.

'What aren't you hungry? Is something wrong?' Dolores asked a second time.

'The superior chief has sent Inspector Rios to Llueso to take command.'

'Why?'

'He reckons I'm not doing a good enough job.'

'Then he is an even bigger fool than I have always thought!'

'And I'm to appear before a hearing, charged with inefficiency and being insultingly rude to an important English lady.'

'Because you couldn't catch her?' Juan asked.

'Up to your bedroom,' Dolores snapped.

Juan angrily pushed back his chair, stamped over to the stairs and up them.

Alvarez emptied his glass. 'All I did was ask her questions which had to be asked. But she's the kind of person who expects you to bow before you speak. I'm convinced she has the key to the problem, but if I'm not allowed to question her again, I'll never know if I'm right.'

'Of course you are,' Dolores said loyally.

Rios had been in Llueso only four days, but to Alvarez it seemed more like four months. Everything he did was questioned and criticised; time and again, he was reminded that the Manual of Procedure demanded this was done that way and that was done this way; crime was solved by facts, not fanciful suppositions; his manner of work was suggestive of an inbuilt laziness; his liking for alcohol was a sign of moral as well as physical degeneracy.

He parked in the shade of a tree and made his way toward Club Llueso along roads crowded with tourists whose aimless wanderings irritatingly caused him to zigzag. He had almost reached the club building when a cry of 'Inspector' halted him. He turned to face Laura Gerrard, her expression as indicative of worry as had been her tone.

'Good morning, Señora.'

'Thank God we've met. I must talk to you.'

'Then since I was about to have a coffee, perhaps you'll join me?'

Her concern was such, she didn't thank him, merely nodded.

He led the way inside and across to a window table. 'It's a pleasant custom to have a coñac with the morning coffee, Señora, so may I get you one?'

'No.' She realised she had been rudely abrupt. 'Thank you, but I won't.'

'Would you like a coffee cortado, solo, or con leche?'

'I don't mind.'

Alvarez crossed to the bar and gave his order. 'So you've found company,' said the bartender, with a knowing wink.

'It's work,' Alvarez replied shortly.

'She's not young enough to get it all off without you having to try?'

'You've a mind like a sewer.'

'I adjust my conversation to the customer.' He started the espresso machine, then with bad-tempered small-mindedness poured a normal-sized brandy.

Alvarez carried the two coffees and one brandy on a tray to the table, passed one cup and saucer to Laura. She poured the contents of a packet of sugar into her cup, then began to screw the paper between thumb and forefinger.

'Something is troubling you greatly, Señora,' he said, as he settled opposite her.

'When I saw you ... I've been going crazy with worry and you've always seemed so kind, I thought...'

'You thought what?'

'Maybe you would help. That beastly man keeps questioning my husband and making it obvious he thinks he is a murderer. Charles explains again and again he'd absolutely no idea Dora had much money or that she'd leave anything to him, but Rios just won't believe that and one can see him inwardly sneering. He even suggested perhaps Charles had been caught by a peeper in a compromising situation and that he'd killed the peeper to prevent my knowing about it. Why can't the man understand what sort of a person Charles is?'

'I fear he judges everyone by himself.'

'You understand, don't you?'

'I like to think so.'

'You cannot begin to believe Charles killed Dora and that man?'

'I am certain he did not.'

'Then for God's sake make Rios realise how stupid he's being.'

He drank some brandy, poured what remained into the cup. 'Señora, he is now in charge of the case and unlikely to take any heed of what I say.'

She stared at him for several seconds, then said bitterly: 'In other words, you won't try to help. You all stick together.' She dropped the now fragmented pieces of paper into her saucer. 'I must seem very stupid, asking for your help. But a wife becomes stupid when her husband is wrongly suspected of murder and in danger of being put into a Spanish jail.'

'Señora, I certainly do not think you stupid. Of course I will speak to Inspector

Rios and try to convince him that your husband would never commit murder, whatever the circumstances, but I do not wish to raise your hopes. Inspector Rios is ... Will you understand if I say that one can show a man a book, one cannot make him read it?'

She reached across the table briefly to touch his arm. 'Forgive me.'

He would have given much to be able to pluck out of the air evidence which would clear her husband and banish from her eyes that expression of desperate anxiety and fear.

Alvarez climbed the stairs, paused to regain his breath and wipe the sweat from his forehead, entered the office. Rios sat at what had been his desk; a rickety old desk had been brought in from another room and that was now his. He sat, grateful for a rest.

'You've been away a long time,' Rios said.

'Have I?'

'You may find the superior chief will ask why you were not here.'

'Is that a roundabout way of saying he phoned? If so, I'll bet you didn't tell him I was out on a case.'

'Since you do not keep a Movements Book, I couldn't say what you were doing.'

'You should have told him, I was having coffee and a coñac with a charming lady.'

'He does not appreciate childish jokes.'

'It is not a joke. I have been enjoying Señora Gerrard's company.'

'Are you incapable of understanding an order? You were told to have no further contact with the case.'

'When she stopped me in the street and invited me to have a coffee with her, should I have rudely spurned her invitation?'

'What did she want?'

'To ask me to explain something to you.'

'What?'

'You've been questioning her husband and making it obvious you believe he's a murderer.'

'So?'

'Señor Gerrard is an English gentleman.'

'You think that guarantees his innocence?'

'In his case, yes.'

'Preferring logic to fantasy, I believe that to someone in great financial difficulties, more than two hundred thousand pounds is a very attractive reward for drowning an old woman. And having murdered once, a second murder becomes much easier.'

'That's to ignore the standards by which a man like him lives.'

'I begin to understand ever more clearly

the many reasons you have never gained promotion.'

Salas phoned as Alvarez was about to leave the office to return home. 'Until the hearing into your conduct, you are suspended from duty. The director-general will appoint a superior chief from the Cuerpo and a colonel from the Guardia to be adjudicators. You are entitled to be represented by an abogado or a notario, should you imagine the expense incurred could prove to be justified.' He rang off.

Twenty-Two

Jaime hurried into the dining-room and sat on the opposite side of the table to Alvarez. He picked up the bottle of wine and filled a glass. 'You look like you've lost the winning lottery ticket.'

'I'm to be given the date for the hearing.'

'What hearing?'

'I told you about it on Tuesday.'

'Can't remember.'

'I'm suspended from duty.'

'Some people get all the luck.'

Some people lacked any sense of compassion. Alvarez drank. Alcohol might be a false comforter, but false comfort could be preferable to true discomfort.

Jaime looked at the bead curtain over the kitchen doorway. 'It's quiet in there. Isn't she back yet?'

'No.'

'Then lunch is likely to be late.'

Alvarez was silent.

'You're a bundle of joy! What's the real

problem? That young bit of foreign goods you're after is still running too fast for you?'

'Can't you understand...? No, I don't suppose you can.'

'Talking about women, guess who we met in the supermarket when I had to carry what Dolores bought. Damned if I know why. Some of the things she wanted were heavy, but it's not far to where the cars are parked.'

Alvarez drained his glass, refilled it.

'The Ortegas. By God, Benito's talking big these days! To listen to him, you'd think he'd bought the whole island. And I can remember when he couldn't rattle two pesetas together. I'll tell you what's the first thing I'd do if I had the money he says he does – I'd trade in Luisa. Married to her, a separate bedroom's a luxury. And Eva's a carbon copy of her mother.' He drank. 'We've got you to blame.'

'Have you?'

'She invited them all to a meal because she reckons Eva can't hope to marry into a good family, not with her looks and manner, so she'll have to make do with anyone who'll ask and you're going to do the asking.'

'Like hell I am!'

'Are you forgetting Manuel? He said he'd never bother to get married because the tourists provided all any man could want, but his mother demanded a grandson and in no time he was married to Magdalena. He still doesn't seem to know how that happened. I reckon women are witches.'

'Then I'd better eat a lot more garlic.'

Isabel and Juan were with friends, so supper was quieter than usual and not much was said before Dolores served Coca de nata.

She gave herself a small portion, picked up spoon and fork, but did not immediately eat. 'Is it all right?'

Since they were unable to judge what mood she was in, both Alvarez and Jaime hastened to assure her that it was the most delicious coca they had ever eaten.

'My mother was a better cook than me, but she used to say I could make a better Coca de nata than she could,' Dolores observed.

'You're wrong and she was right,' Alvarez said.

'What's that?'

'Your mother could not have been a better cook and no one could produce a better coca than this.'

'There is no need to exaggerate,' she said approvingly. 'I think this is what I will serve on Monday.' She turned to Alvarez. 'We met the Ortegas and they are coming to lunch, so make sure you are here.'

'I'm not certain I can be.'

'I am. They will eat nothing but the best, yet even so perhaps they will enjoy my Llengua amb taperes.' She was annoyed when neither of them claimed there could not be the slightest doubt. 'We must serve a good wine. Jaime, you will buy two bottles – perhaps three would be better; Benito has the look of a man who enjoys the table.'

'I suppose nothing less than hundred-euro bottles will be good enough?'

'As my mother had reason to remark, "A man will often try to conceal his emptiness with stupidity." '

'You said you wanted good wine.'

'If I even once receive what I want, I will become a fortunate woman. Enrique, you will wear a suit when they are here.'

'In this heat?'

'Whatever the temperature. When one entertains important guests, one does not dishonour them by appearing like a tramp.'

'What if one doesn't mind if one dishonours them?'

'You will wear a suit.'

Alvarez leaned over and opened the right-hand door of the sideboard, brought out a bottle of Soberano. He poured himself a drink, passed the bottle across to Jaime, who made certain her gaze was not fixed on him as he helped himself.

'Son Estar is a very noble possessió,' she remarked.

'I've been told by more than one person that the soil's very poor,' Alvarez said.

'Many opinions are expressed by people who know nothing of what they talk about.'

'One of the men who told me was working there right up until the place was sold.'

'Disposessed tenants make poor judges.'

'The house is in bad shape.'

'Money will turn it into a palace.'

'Water might become a problem with the drop in the water-table.'

'New wells can be bored.'

'Only with permission.'

'The owner of Son Estar will never be refused permission.'

Alvarez gave up trying to denigrate the attractions of the estate.

'Benito and Luisa are naturally very fond of Eva,' Dolores observed, 'and they will make certain that when they die, the government will not be able to steal a peseta. Eva will inherit everything. The man who marries her will be rich indeed.'

'And paying for every crumb she lets drop,' Alvarez muttered, forgetting how keen her hearing could be.

'You are suggesting?'

'From all accounts, she's already much like her mother.'

'Fortunate is the daughter who resembles her mother and not her father.'

'Except when the mother has the looks of a Gorgon and the warmth of an Arctic wind.'

'Men!' she said, so sharply they started.

'You have to admit...' Alvarez began.

'I will tell you what I have to admit. The shame I endure because my cousin cannot believe he is no longer young and handsome and the women, half his age, whom he lusts after conceal their smiles of contempt at his approach.' She stood. 'I have a headache so you will clear the table and if you want coffee, you will make it for yourselves. Jaime, you can put that bottle of coñac back.' She watched him return it to the sideboard before she made her way upstairs.

Jaime faced Alvarez. 'You're so selfish, you're determined to ruin everybody's life.'

For once, Alvarez found difficulty in falling asleep, because he could not escape mental pictures of his being married to Eva Ortega and suffering the humiliation which visited men whose wives were much richer than they; a humiliation which must become all the more vivid when Luisa was one's mother-in-law. He could, of course, show independence by refusing to turn up at the forthcoming meal. But that would anger Dolores, which would ensure that for days, even weeks, meals would be poor.

Ironically, when he did muffle those fears, distress remained because he remembered his promise to help Laura Gerrard, made because he could not bear to see her suffering so much. How could he have given such a promise when he knew he was forbidden to make any further enquiries and soon was to appear before a tribunal, charged with incompetence, insolence, and anything else Salas could think up?

Mercifully, increasing tiredness eventually dimmed his panicky fears and self-reproach, but it was then, about to fall asleep, he was suddenly jerked wide awake by inspiration – there was a way of escaping both a fate worse than death and honouring an impossible promise.

Twenty-Three

Alvarez and Jaime were enjoying their pre-lunch drinks, Dolores was laying the table, when the phone rang. She put down the cutlery in her hand, straightened up. 'Does it occur to either of you to answer that? Does a piglet look forward to Christmas?' She hurried out.

Jaime accepted the opportunity to refill his glass.

She returned. 'The superior chief wants to talk to you, Enrique. It was a man who spoke and told me this, not the woman with the manners of the superior chief. Has she been sacked?'

'I don't think so. I expect she needed a relief and one of the cabos is temporarily doing her job.'

He hurried through to the front room and raised his voice as he said over the phone: 'Alvarez speaking, Señor.'

'And this is the director-general who's awarding you crossed turnips for being a lying bastard.'

'But Señor, I don't think I can,' he said, speaking still more loudly.

'And I'm dead certain you can't.'

'It's just that I have a very important personal matter.'

'Let's have her name so I can warn her what kind of an s... you are.'

'Of course I understand personal matters cannot be allowed to interfere with work.'

'You mean, you don't allow work to interfere with your personal matters.'

'I wouldn't dream of disobeying an order, Señor.'

'Or consider obeying one.'

'Yes, Señor, I understand.'

'That you owe me a slap-up meal at Bona Cepa for this.'

He returned to the dining-room and sat. He tried to look thoroughly downcast.

'Has something gone wrong?' Dolores asked.

'Not exactly, but I am bitterly disappointed.'

'Why?'

'That was to tell me I have to fly to England to pursue investigations into the death of Señorita Coates.'

Jaime, who had been about to drink, held the glass in front of his mouth. 'You told me only yesterday you'd been suspended—'

Alvarez hurriedly cut in. 'That I was worried I would be. Thankfully, I was wrong.'

'I'm sure you said...'

'That Rios was being his usual unpleasant self.'

Dolores stared at Jaime, then at Alvarez. 'When do you have to fly to England?'

'Monday morning.'

'You have forgotten the Ortegas are coming here for a meal on Monday?'

'Of course not.'

'Then why did you not say it was impossible for you to go until Tuesday?'

'I tried to get out of it – didn't you hear me? But I can't argue too hard with Salas and he was adamant I had to do as he said.'

She stood, marched through to the kitchen.

Jaime drank. 'You did say you'd been suspended.'

'Just forget it, will you?'

Dolores pushed through the bead curtain, stood with arms crossed over her bosom. 'It was not the usual woman who spoke to me.'

'So you said,' Alvarez replied.

'It was a man.'

'You mentioned that as well.'

'He sounded as if he was trying not to laugh.'

'Perhaps he'd just heard a good joke.'

'Since it has always been that woman in the past, why did not another woman take over her job?'

'I wouldn't know. Anyway, it's a time of sexual equality so where's the difference?'

'As if a man could ever be the equal of a woman!' She stared suspiciously at him for several more seconds. 'You have not been suspended from duty as Jaime understood you to have said?'

'He got muddled up.'

'That's right,' Jaime said hastily. 'I misunderstood him.'

'Or misunderstood what you were supposed to have heard?'

Alvarez said. 'If I had been suspended, they wouldn't now be sending me to England, would they?'

She returned to the kitchen. It had been a close-run thing, Alvarez thought, especially as she held that whenever a man had a ready answer to explain his actions, he was lying.

Little provoked so much fear in Alvarez's mind as flying. As an altophobe, he dreaded heights; as a logical man, he knew nothing heavier than air could fly unless it was covered in feathers. Only several brandies –

the stewardess seemed to become increasingly reluctant to serve him – enabled him to survive the two hours waiting for the engines to fail, the wings to collapse, the tail to fracture, sudden decompression to suck him out on his last, featherless journey...

As he left the plane, he was tempted to bend down and kiss the floor of the connecting rig, but that was too dirty, so once in the main airport hall, he bought himself a brandy. It was not the gesture of heartfelt gratitude he intended. He had forgotten how absurdly expensive a drink in England was.

As the taxi drove along the narrow, winding lanes, through countryside so green the colour appeared false after the browns of Mallorca, the meter seemed to have gone into overdrive and Alvarez began to think he might be making this journey because he had panicked unnecessarily. It was the age of women's domination, when the law supported them in every field they chose, but it hadn't yet demanded a man be forced to marry at a woman's will rather than his own. Yet had he stayed on the island and not been present when the Ortegas were guests, Dolores might well have decided that endless meals would consist of boiled chickpeas with no rich sauce to disguise their flavour.

'Nearly there,' said the driver.

In the field to the right, two magnificently coloured cock pheasants were sparring, their thoughts on the nearby hen pheasants, not the first of October. As they passed out of sight, Alvarez assured himself that it was ridiculous to worry about the cost of this taxi ride, or to balance that against his escaping Eva. The prime reason for this trip to England was an altruistic one. He was pursing the hundred-to-one chance he could uncover proof which would release Laura Gerrard from the fear which gripped her. Yet – as the meter ticked on – he could not stop himself wondering if it had ever been remotely possible he might prove Gerrard's innocence by this visit? Where did he start a search for something he couldn't identify or define?

'Here you are, then, mate. Looks like open day.'

He paid the excessive amount of money recorded on the meter and added a tip which he considered over-generous, but which made the driver's lips curl. As the car drove away, he studied Stayforth House, some thousand yards from where he stood. *Country Life* would have termed it a smaller country house, but to him it was an English

mansion. Brick-built, symmetrically proportioned, it had tall sash windows on the lower
and upper floors and four dormer windows
above these; in the centre of the tiled roof
was a belvedere with arched windows and
corners picked out in white stone. The
grounds were extensive; the lawns looked to
be of bowling-green smoothness, the flower
beds were filled with colour, the yews
clipped into the shape of animals were
topiary art, and there were several female
statues to add further interest. Beyond the
ha-ha was rolling countryside and woods.
Small wonder, he thought, that when the
Gerrards had spoken about the estate, it had
been with pride and regret. Had he been
Charles Gerrard, time could never lessen his
bitter sense of injustice that no part of this
was his merely because he was the younger
son.

The main wrought-iron gates were closed;
at the much smaller side gate, he was asked
for five pounds entrance fee. His surprise
must have shown, because the woman seated at the table tartly told him all entrance
money was donated to charity, thanks to the
generosity of Lady Gerrard.

He walked around the gardens, marvelling
at the work and cost involved in keeping
them in such pristine condition. A notice

outside the very large walled garden announced this was out of bounds to visitors. A man was working by the entrance and Alvarez engaged him in conversation and explained he was from Mallorca and how interesting it was to see what fruit and vegetables were grown in so cold and inhospitable a climate. He could project an easy warmth of character and soon was asked into the kitchen garden. Liberal praise for the quality of what he saw, frequent exclamations of surprise at the fruit on the espalier trees, soon had the gardener speaking freely; a deliberate misidentification of yellow tomatoes enabled him to refer to the Gerrards and mention what a pleasant couple they were.

'Aye, Mr Charles and his missus are fine. And if they were here instead of her ladyship...' He became silent.

'Lady Gerrard seems a very difficult sort of person.'

'Met her, have you?'

'She's staying in her house on the island and I've had to talk to her once or twice.'

'Been a problem, has there? I mean, what with you being a policeman.'

'There has. And she's caused trouble objecting to some of the things I had to say to her.'

The gardener bent down and inspected a slug trap laced with beer. 'She's bloody good at objecting.' He straightened up. 'Comes and tells me all what's wrong with the garden when she don't know nothing about nowt. They say in the house that she's a right royal ... Don't do to bite the hand what feeds you.'

'But it can be very satisfying.'

The gardener's deeply lined face creased as he laughed. 'That's right enough! The gentry always complains, but they know how to do that, she don't. To be frank, I never understood what made Sir Jerome marry her instead of one of his own kind. All right, she'd the looks and likely gave him his money's worth in bed, but he could have had all that on the side, like most of 'em do. It wouldn't surprise me if he'd asked himself more than once why he married her. And if he ever suspected...'

'Suspected what?'

'Shouldn't rightly say.'

'A policeman is like a priest, his lips are sealed.'

The gardener moved forward several paces, bent down to examine a line of lettuces and spoke while remaining bending. 'Sir Jerome was away on a business trip, soon after they was married, and a man came visiting more often than Sir Jerome would have wished. A smooth bastard, being French.'

'Are you suggesting they had an affair?'

The gardener finally straightened up. 'I ain't said nothing.'

'I haven't heard anything.'

'Tell you what, it's time for a coffee; care for some?'

'I would indeed.'

Whether what he drank in the wooden potting shed was coffee, Alvarez was not certain. He braved himself to finish what was in the cup, refused with thanks the offer of a refill, remarked he'd been hoping to look over the house because Señor Gerrard had spoken so enthusiastically about it, but he understood the house wasn't open to the public.

'They tried to get her to allow it because it could bring in more money, but she wasn't having that. But there's no problem, not with you knowing Mr Charles. I'll have a word with Mrs Dobbs and she'll show you around, then you can go back and tell Mr Charles how the place looks. Though maybe that's not such a good idea. Won't make him happy, thinking of her and that little snipe of a son living here.'

Mrs Dobbs was tall, thin, and angular, but

possessed of a warmer character than her appearance suggested and she agreed to show Alvarez around the house. She asked him how Mr and Mrs Charles were and would he give them her regards when he next saw them. They went out of the kitchen and along a passage to a door lined with green beige. 'The iron curtain,' she said, with a laugh.

'I'm sorry?'

'The end of our world and the beginning of hers. I don't suppose she's come through once since she's lived here. Never understood she could show an interest in what goes on without us trying to become familiar.'

Beyond, there was for him a world from television. Large rooms with moulded ceilings, fireplaces with carved marble mantelpieces, extravagant curtains, magnificent carpets, antique furniture with glowing patina, display cabinets filled with gold, silver, ivory, and porcelain, paintings by old masters, a library with shelves filled with matching leather-bound volumes...

'This is the oldest bit of family history,' she said in the blue room, as she came to a stop by a rosewood display table with splayed legs.

He looked through the glass top at the

black velvet-lined interior in which lay fourteen heart-shaped gold lockets, each with a diamond in the centre, its gold chain artistically arranged, and by its side a small tag on which was written a name and a Roman numeral or numerals.

'The first is from the seventeenth century when Sir Peter Gerrard was born, not that he was the first baronet then; the title wasn't created until twenty-two years later. The story goes, he was a sickly child and likely to die and his mother was so distraught, she had the locket made and put his hair in it so that if he died she'd always have a little of him close to her heart. He lived to be seventy-nine and since then a similar locket has been made each time an heir is born. It's become a family superstition – provided there's a locket, the heir won't die early. Sir Fergus, Sir Jerome's young son, is the fifteenth baronet and it's his locket at the bottom on the right.'

The lockets seemed to have a familiar shape, yet unable to place why this should be, he dismissed the possibility as meaningless. Because his work had trained him to check everything where possible, he automatically and without conscious thought, counted the lockets. 'There are only fourteen.'

'Not many notice that. Sir Jerome's locket disappeared some years back.' After a moment, she said: 'George said as you're a detective in Spain?'

'I am, yes.'

'Then there can't be no harm in saying. I wasn't here at the time, but I've been told the talk was, it was stolen by an employee. Seems she was suspected, but Lady Gerrard wouldn't have the police called in, said it wasn't worth the fuss and bother. She couldn't understand what the loss meant to Sir Jerome, of course, her not really being of the family. I've often thought, maybe it wasn't an ordinary theft. Women get funny ideas sometimes. I mean, they become so sentimentally possessive of someone they've looked after, they begin to think they've a right to a memento of him. And when she left, she'd been working as nursemaid to Sir Fergus.'

'What was her name?'

'Dora. Don't remember her surname.'

'Coates?'

'That's right. But how did you guess?'

'She visited Lady Gerrard just before she died.'

'Well I never! And you say she's dead?'

'Drowned in Llueso Bay.'

'Poor woman. But we all have to die, it's

just the way it happens that's different.'

Hardly comforting words, he thought, as he casually looked back at the lockets; and then, although he wasn't trying to provoke his memory, it responded. He had found a similar one in Dora Coates's hotel bedroom. He had come to Stayforth House in the hopes he would discover something important concerning the Gerrards, Dora Coates, and Colin Short; all he had learned was that Dora had stolen a locket when she had worked for the Gerrards. As any Mallorquin who had lived through the troubled years could have told him, 'Hope never did fill an empty belly.'

Twenty-Four

Alvarez sat at the kitchen table and miserably accepted that very soon a superior chief and a colonel would sit in judgement of him. The more Senior an officer, the stronger his sense of traditional values – one must believe a lady of rank, disbelieve a mere inspector. He would be dismissed the force. No pension, nothing to show for all his years of hard, faithful service; his life reduced to a minimum standard; a bottle of the cheapest wine, a purchase which had to be considered before it was made...

His bitter ruminations were suddenly banished by a revelation from on high. Mrs Dobbs had planted in his mind the belief Dora Coates had taken the locket because she longed to have a memento of the child she'd helped to rear. But it was Sir Jerome's locket which had been stolen, not his son's. So the motive for the taking had been plain theft, the desire for a memento of the whole family rather than of the child, or a mistake

– she had meant to take Fergus's locket. The last might seem the least likely, remembering each locket had a name tag by it, but she might have been under such emotional stress – an honest woman knowing she was committing theft, but unable to resist the urge – that she had not had the wit to check what she was taking. As to which was the correct answer, he didn't give a damn. He refilled his glass. There was one small glimmer of light amidst the darkness. Before he was ignominiously thrown out of the Cuerpo, he could make certain the locket found in Dora Coates's handbag was returned to Stayforth House so that tradition was once more intact.

Rios said: 'I told you to report here in order to give you a message from the superior chief.'

'It didn't occur to you to phone me at home?'

'The superior chief said I was to speak to you face to face so that there could be no chance of your suggesting you had misheard because of poor telephone lines. You are reminded you are to attend the hearing into your conduct and are to report to headquarters in Palma at twelve hundred hours. Is that understood?'

'Yes.'

'I'm off now, to question Señor Gerrard.'

'Again?'

'However clever a man thinks himself, there is always a time when he forgets what he has previously said.'

'But the interrogator remembers, because he is so much cleverer?'

Rios left.

Unaware of the irony of remaining in the office when he was suspended from duty and so free to leave and do what he wanted, Alvarez sat in the chair behind his desk. He stared at the unshuttered window. He was still convinced Lady Gerrard was in some way connected with the deaths of Dora Coates and Jiminez – so that his questioning of her and his examination of her financial affairs had been justified – but if asked to provide a scintilla of proof of this conviction, he would have to stay silent. Would the two judges, could the two judges, understand that she had complained of his behaviour because she was a vindictive woman; that she exaggerated whenever it suited her to do so ... But money and position dulled most men's minds.

The phone rang.

'There's a woman asking for you,' the duty cabo said. 'Leastwise, I think that's her problem. She doesn't speak anything but English, keeps saying your name.'

'What's hers?'

'Gemma Hearn,' the cabo answered, mispronouncing both words badly.

'Never heard of her.'

'She must be a recent contact since she doesn't look very pregnant.'

'Your sense of humour suggests considerable immaturity.' He replaced the receiver. Then wondered why he hadn't said that whatever the woman wanted, it wasn't his pigeon since he was not longer actively working. He sighed. A sense of duty clung to one like fleas to a dying dog.

When he saw Gemma by the duty desk, he accepted that he had met her, but couldn't think when or where. 'Good morning, Señorita.'

'Thank God you've arrived! I was beginning to wonder if I'd ever make the policeman understand I wanted to speak to you.'

'I'm afraid not everyone speaks English. How can I help you?'

'Colin asked me to see you.'

The name identified her and he wondered how he could have failed to do so before – perhaps it was because she was wearing clothes. 'Let's go along to an interview-room, where it will be much quieter.' And the cabo wouldn't be looking at her with lascivious interest.

Once they were seated in the small, rather airless room, she said: 'Before he left, Colin asked the people in the hotel for his aunt's things they had in the safe, but they wouldn't hand them over without your authorisation. He wants me to ask you to tell them it's OK to give the things to me.'

'Señor Short has left the island?'

'He was called back unexpectedly, which is why he hasn't come here himself.' She smiled. 'I told Colin I wasn't going to have you think I was trying to pull a fast one, so I made him write out a request.' She opened her small handbag and brought out a single sheet of hotel notepaper, folded in the centre, leaned across to hand it to him.

He read what was written. He looked up. 'I'm afraid there is a problem.'

'Why's that?'

'The cash, the travellers' cheques, and the locket cannot yet be handed to you.'

'But Colin said he particularly wanted to have the locket because it was of such sentimental value to Dora and therefore to him. He'll be very upset if I can't give it to him.'

Alvarez's thoughts quickened. 'Did he say why it was of such sentimental value?'

'It belonged to Dora's mother and was the

only thing of hers Dora had. Can't you let him have it?'

Not until he knew whether or not it was the solution to many questions as well as being stolen property. 'There is something I must establish before I can release it.'

'You won't let me have it now?'

'I'm sorry.'

'Then you will make certain it's safe?'

'Of course. When are you returning to England, Señorita?'

'Tomorrow morning, early; too early for me.' Again that quick smile.

'Obviously, you are seeing Señor Short again?'

'Yes. We ... we enjoyed each other's company.' Then in a rush of shared confidences, she added: 'I told him I'd always dreamed of going to Barbados because when I was young, I'd read it was an earthly heaven, and he promised we'd go there as soon as I could get some more time off work. We'll spend days and days lying in the sun, swimming and snorkeling in the sea, staring at palm trees, and drinking daiquiris ... Inspector, I'm sorry, but I must rush because I've promised to drive a charming couple – she's sadly crippled, yet always cheerful – out to the lighthouse and a picnic on Parelona beach.'

A possibility suddenly occurred to him. 'You've hired a car for today, Señorita?' he asked casually.

'I've had one all the time I've been here. Which turned out to be an awful waste, because Colin had one as well.'

'So Señor Short was able to borrow yours when that was necessary?'

She stared at him with sharp surprise. 'How did you know...' She stopped.

'Yes?'

'It doesn't matter.'

'I think perhaps it does.'

'Look, I couldn't be certain.'

'If I knew what happened, I might be able to judge.'

'I don't think I want to tell you.'

'I'm afraid you must.'

She fidgeted with a fold in her frock.

'You couldn't be certain of what, Señorita?'

'That it was ... One night, I had a head and went to bed early. Later, something woke me and I had the frightening feeling that someone was or had been in my bedroom. Of course, I switched on the light; there was no one there, so I decided it just had to have been a bad dream and I went back to sleep. But in the morning, I looked in my handbag for a handkerchief and it

300

seemed to me that everything had been moved around.'

'So what did you believe explained this?'

'I couldn't think. I spoke to Colin about it and he said I obviously didn't keep my handbag nearly as tidily as I thought and no one could have been in my room. Only he spoke so forcefully, I had the impression ... well, that he was trying to make me believe what he said... Anyway, I asked him if he'd been in my room that night and he just laughed. But when I went to my car again, I was certain it had been driven somewhere.'

'Why was that?'

'When I'd last parked it, I'd noticed the final four figures of the mileometer – kilometer? – were the month and days of my birthday. But they weren't any longer.'

'Could you have driven somewhere and forgotten the fact when you mentally compared numbers?'

'There was almost sixty difference.'

'When was this?'

'A little time back.'

'You can't be more precise?'

'Not really.'

'Do you still have the car?'

'I'm returning it this afternoon.'

'Which firm did you rent it from?'

'The hotel arranged that.'

He stood. 'Thank you for your help.'

She hesitated, then said: 'I don't really understand why you won't give me the locket; why you've been asking so many questions.'

'Señorita, I fear that in my job, one becomes very curious, more often than not for no good reason.'

He escorted her down to the main entrance and said goodbye. Back in his room, he phoned Hotel Monterray and spoke to Diego. 'What car-hire firm are you using this year?'

'I'm not certain.'

'Scared I'll whistle when I learn the commission they pay you? Come on, a name.'

'Garaje Llueso.'

He checked what was the firm's number, dialled it. 'You've hired a car to Señorita Hearn and the hiring comes to an end later today. Take another car to the hotel right away and tell her it's to replace the one she's been using.'

'But if she's returning hers...'

'Make up some story about suspension; being a woman, she won't know what you're talking about. Hold the car until I say what to do with it.'

'Who's going pay for this?'

'You are.'

'Then suppose I tell you to get stuffed.'

'I'll be along to look over your premises and cars and it wouldn't be surprising if I found so many faults you'd have to close down.'

'What a nasty sod you can be!'

'It's gratifying to learn I'm doing my job well.' He replaced the receiver, leaned over and opened the right-hand drawer of the desk, brought out the bottle of brandy and a glass. As the poet Valverde had written, wine embraced health and comforted affliction, gloried success and dimmed failure.

He drank. He'd mournfully judged his trip to England to have been a complete waste of money and time, yet now he knew he had learned something which at the time had seemed unimportant, yet which might prove to be very important. Short had told Gemma his mother had given him the locket, yet in truth it had been stolen from Stayforth House. Why had he lied?

Twenty-Five

Alvarez held the receiver to his ear with one hand, drummed the fingers of the other on the desk as tension tied a granny knot in his stomach.

'Are you there?' asked the man from Vehicles.

Did the fool think he'd gone for a walk? 'What's the result?'

'There's not been time to examine the Ford Fiesta.'

'What are you doing – teaching chickens to clean their teeth? This is priority.'

'According to the docket, it's a routine job.'

'I said...'

'You know as well as me that the only time priority is actually given to a job, it's when a comisario or the superior chief says so.'

'Salas said so.'

'Give me his written order and I'll believe you.'

'I have to have the results as quickly as possible.'

'Not a hope. Half the cars on the island have come in for examination. You'll be lucky if your job starts before the weekend.'

'But I've spoken to the Institute and they've promised any traces which reach them before too late in the afternoon will be examined immediately.'

'Maybe they knew that's a promise they won't have to keep.'

'Suppose I was to slip across a ten-euro note?'

'You reckon we're all down-and-outs?'

'Twenty euros.'

'You're lucky I'm soft-hearted.'

Yet again, Alvarez checked the time. A watched kettle never boiled, but a watched watch raced. Would, could the deadline set by the Institute be met? Failure became ever more certain; his theories were based on quicksand; his hopes were phantoms; his remaining time in the Cuerpo was number-ed in hours. What remained but a noose, a gun, a hosepipe led from the exhaust to the interior of the Ibiza, a one-way walk into the sea?

The phone rang. A woman reported that certain intimate articles had been stolen from an outside washing line where they had been hung to dry and she was certain the thief was the man who lived along the road and ... He slammed down the receiver in an uncharacteristic display of curt bad manners.

What could be more futile than waiting for something which was not going to happen? The workers at Vehicles were lazy and incompetent and couldn't be bothered to check the Fiesta to discover if there were any traces which might prove the body of Jiminez had once been carried in it.

The phone rang. Grains of sand and one woollen fibre had been found in the boot of the Fiesta and these were being taken immediately to the Institute by a man from Trafico who had volunteered to make the journey. Those who worked in Vehicles were painstakingly thorough and full of initiative, the men from Trafico were loyal comrades.

He phoned the Institute and spoke to an assistant who said they had a moment before received the fibre and sand and comparison checks would begin immediately; however, it could already be stated it was unlikely the sand would offer any qualities which could provide meaningful comparisons.

Time passed, his tension increased. The phone rang yet again. Since the tests appeared to be so important, the speaker had dropped all other work and carried them out. He could now say without qualification that the fibre found in the boot of the Fiesta matched in all respects the fibre found on the body of Jiminez. The sand offered no chance of comparison.

Alvarez replaced the receiver. If Dora Coates had been murdered or allowed to drown when she could have been saved, Short would have been the prime suspect had not his lack of any motive, the fact that he seemingly benefited only when she was alive, seemed to mark his innocence. The only motive for Short's murder of Jiminez had been attempted blackmail, yet blackmail over what if not the circumstances of Dora's drowning? Before his trip to England, Alvarez could not have suggested answers even if convinced beyond doubt that Short was the murderer; now, he thought he knew what they were. But the only way to make certain was to take the risk of being wrong, knowing that if he were, Salas would order him to be beheaded before he was dismissed from the Cuerpo.

It was the morning of the hearing, Alvarez went into the kitchen as Dolores walked in through the outside doorway. She put a loosely secured, brown-paper package on

307

the table, unwound the ends. 'I bought the ensaimadas from Ca Na Rosalia because they make the best ones these days.'

He thanked her warmly. Because she was so worried on his behalf, knowing how much he liked a good ensaimada, she had cycled right across the village. There were times when one had to forget how sharp her tongue could be.

Twenty minutes later, he phoned the bank and spoke to Fortega. 'I'd be grateful if you'd do me a favour...'

'You've got to be making a bloody awful joke! A favour! Do you a favour after the trouble you caused with the last one you wanted? Lady Gerrard created so much hell, we had an investigating officer out from Palma, trying to identify who had given you details of that woman's accounts.'

'But he didn't name you?'

'You think I'd still be working here if he had?'

'Then there's no harm done.'

'That's ripe! You weren't involved, so never worry about anyone else; doesn't matter what I went through. I'm not doing you another favour, not if you get down on hands and knees and beg.'

'It's really important or I wouldn't bother you.'

'Just forget it.'

'I need to know if Lady Gerrard has withdrawn a large sum in cash since the twenty-first of last month.'

There was a silence.

'Did you hear?'

'I heard. And I'm asking myself, is the man insanely simple, or simply insane.'

'It's vital I know.'

'To me, it's vital you don't know.'

'You weren't identified last time, so they won't be able to nail you this time.'

'Quite right, they won't, because you're not even learning what the time is from me.' He cut the connection.

Alvarez dialled again. 'You rang off before I could warn you.'

'Warn me about what?' Fortega asked angrily.

'That I have to have the information to complete my investigation. If I can't finish it, I can't guarantee I won't be forced to disclose who gave me the information in the first instance.'

'Has anyone said you're the complete bastard?'

'As a matter of fact, someone said something of the sort not so long ago.'

Fifteen minutes later, Alvarez learned that on the 22nd of the previous month, Lady

Gerrard had had twenty thousand Swiss francs transferred from a bank in Zurich, subsequently withdrawing twelve thousand euros in cash.

He thanked Fortega for the information.

'If you get run over by a bus, you'll hear me laughing all the way to the nearest bar.'

Filipe opened the front door of Ca'n Jerome and stared with surprise at Alvarez. 'You're the last person I expected to see here! Don't you know the plague's more welcome?'

'I have to have another word with Lady Gerrard.'

'She's in such a filthy temper, Ana and I have finally given in our notice.'

'How did she accept that?'

'Like the fishwife she is ... You still want to talk to her?'

'Yes.'

'You must be a masochist. She's out by the pool.'

Heloise was swimming from the deep to the shallow end; when she saw Alvarez, she stopped and stood, the water reaching halfway up her shapely thighs, her brightly coloured bikini offering little more than token modesty. Bitch that she was, Alvarez still knew brief desire. Man was born at a disadvantage.

'What are you doing here?' she demanded furiously.

'I'd like a word, Lady Gerrard.'

'Get out.'

'It will be to your advantage...'

'How dare you try to tell me what's to my advantage. Filipe, show him out immediately.'

'Lady Gerrard...'

'Filipe, phone the consul.'

'What, please?' Felipe said.

'My God, if I'd known you can't speak the language.' She faced Alvarez once more. 'You will pay for this insolence, I promise you that. My complaint will be sent to the highest level...'

'I am here to talk about a locket.'

She stared at him, her expression suddenly strained.

'In which is a lock of Sir Jerome Gerrard's hair, taken when he was a very young boy.'

'I don't know what you're talking about.' Her tone was no longer arrogant and abrasive. She slowly walked through the water to the steps, climbed them, crossed to the pool patio and a chair.

Alvarez moved a second chair and sat. 'On the contrary, you know only too well. That locket has fuelled the blackmail you have suffered for many years, first at the hands of

311

Dora Coates and then her nephew, Colin Short. Short has begun to blackmail you far more heavily than she did, hasn't he? He understood the full potential value of the locket and that was why he tried again and again to persuade his aunt to increase the money she demanded, but she wouldn't; as strange as this might seem, perhaps her conscience prevented her asking for what she considered to be too much. I am now convinced it was conscience which persuaded her to will her ill-gotten money to Señor Gerrard – an act of delayed contrition, one could say. Her refusal to agree to do what he wanted ensured her death because he has no such conscience or ability to appreciate the benefits of moderation, as you have discovered when having to find ever more money to meet his demands.'

'I don't understand what you're talking about. No one's blackmailing me.'

'Then to whom did you pay the twelve thousand euros you've very recently withdrawn from your bank?'

She made a sound at the back of her throat that resembled the mew of a cat.

'Why were you being blackmailed?'

'I've just told you I wasn't.'

'Was it because Sir Jerome was not the father of your son?'

She struggled to sound angry, not frightened. 'How dare you suggest such a disgusting lie.'

'Señorita Coates was your lady's maid and this provided her with reason to know you were not pregnant before Sir Jerome went abroad on a business trip. You had an affair with a Frenchman...'

'That's a filthy lie!'

'The staff at Stayforth House were not blind.'

'They've made it up because they all resent me; they're the worst possible snobs; they despise me because I'm from the same background as they are.'

'It was a casual affair, but with an irony that is not unusual, you became pregnant. Circumstances allowed you to make out Sir Jerome was the father and therefore when he died in an accident, Fergus inherited the estate. But it should have passed to Mr Charles Gerrard, who became the legal fourteenth baronet.'

'You can't prove a thing.'

'The locket can. Which is why Señorita Coates stole it. DNA tests can be conducted on the lock of Sir Jerome's hair it contains and the results compared with the DNA of you and your son; the results will prove beyond doubt that Fergus is not Sir

Jerome's son.'

'You haven't got the locket...'

'Then Colin Short never told you that when I searched Señorita Coates's hotel room after her death, I found the locket as well as the blackmail money she had obtained from you after arriving in Port Llueso? The money and the locket are still under my custody.'

Minutes passed before she said: 'I don't suppose you're very well paid?'

'It is true, I am not well paid in comparison to many. But it is your misfortune, as well as mine, that I try to be honest.'

She began to cry.

He had expected to enjoy deep satisfaction from destroying her arrogance, but as he watched the tears slide down her smooth, creamy cheeks, he was annoyed to find himself feeling sorry for her.

He climbed out of the car and as he walked towards the front door of Ca'n Dento, he tried and failed to enter the mind of someone suddenly given the right to leave poverty and enjoy great luxury.

Laura opened the door. 'It's you.' Conscious her greeting had been far from welcoming, she said quickly: 'Do come in, Inspector. It's nice to see you again.' After a brief pause, she added: 'I suppose you want a word with Charles?'

'And with you, Señora.'

'Have you...' She angrily shook her head, stepped to one side to let him enter.

As he walked from the kitchen on to the vine-covered patio, Gerrard came to his feet. 'Good morning, Señor.'

'Let's vainly hope so. We were about to enjoy the excellent morning custom of coffee with a brandy, so do join us before you explain why you're here. Bad news should always be allowed to rust a little.'

'Perhaps it would be better if I speak first.'

'I doubt it, but something suggests you're going to.'

They sat.

'I have come here after speaking to Lady Gerrard.'

'A veritable Daniel!' Gerrard said ironically.

'I explained that I knew she had been suffering blackmail for many years.'

'Good God! Blackmail over what?'

'The fact that Sir Jerome was not the father of her son.'

They stared at him, their faces drawn tight by shock.

'You are serious?' Gerrard finally asked.

'It will, of course, require DNA tests to

315

prove that fact, but there can be no doubt.'

She spoke to her husband. 'Then ... Then you were Jerome's heir, not Fergus? And the estate's yours? Oh, my God!' She began to cry.

Heloise had cried from anger, Laura from joy. No wonder women confounded men, Alvarez thought.

He walked into the dining-room. Jaime was seated at the table and Dolores stood just in front of the bead curtain; they stared at him with concern.

'Sweet Mary, where have you been?' Dolores finally asked. 'Time and again, the superior chief has phoned and rudely demanded to know where you were and when I couldn't answer, became even more obnoxious. He has said that if you don't arrive in Palma within the next half-hour to attend the hearing, he'll order the Guardia to arrest you. Why aren't you there?'

'I forgot about the hearing.'

'You forgot? So where is your memory – left in a bar?'

The phone rang.

'That's him,' she said. Her brief anger gave way to concern. 'Shall I say you've been involved in a car accident? Or maybe you've fallen and been knocked unconscious?'

'I'll speak to him. And there's no need to worry.'

'No need, when you've lost the few wits you once had?'

He went through to the front room.

Salas spoke with such anger that he was barely comprehensible. His authority had been publicly flouted; he had been humiliated by having to apologise to a fellow superior chief and a colonel from the Guardia for the insolent stupidity of his inspector.

'Señor, perhaps I might explain? It became clear to me that it was necessary to be certain of all the facts in order to pass these on to you before I appeared before the hearing, no matter what delay that caused, for fear that otherwise my answers to some of the questions put to me by the adjudicators might well make them mistakenly believe that although you were in command, you remained ignorant of certain vital facts.

'Lady Gerrard – I am not certain if she remains that – no longer has any relevant cause for complaint. And without a cause, there can be no justification for a hearing, can there, Señor?'

Salas did not answer.

'I understand from what you said and didn't say a moment ago, the adjudicators

317

expressed themselves in robust terms because I failed to appear before them. Knowing how loyally you always defend those under your command, I am sure you will be very content to be able to point out to them that they were rather premature in their criticisms and must consider themselves fortunate they did not convene the hearing, since had they done so – now it can be shown to be totally unnecessary – they would publicly have proved themselves to be ill-advised, especially when one remembers that the efficient officer only pursues a course when he can be certain he is fully justified in doing so. Is that not something you have said to me many times, Señor?'

'Yes,' Salas muttered, as if speaking while a nerve gnawed at a wisdom tooth.

'I was only able to reach the truth after travelling to England...'

'What?' he shouted.

'I flew to England.'

'Who authorised the journey?'

'No one.'

'This time you've gone too far...'

'Señor, since I was suspended from duty, it was difficult to know who could authorise my journey. As you have often said to me, an officer in the Cuerpo is expected to use his initiative. I had become certain I might find

the key to unlock the cases concerning Señorita Coates and Jiminez in England, but I had no proof this was so. It was in such circumstances I decided to travel. Since I was successful, I think I may claim I was right to accept that instinct and a feeling can sometimes be of more use than fact. Would you not agree?'

Again, there was no answer.

'Naturally, I had to pay for the journey out of my own pocket. However, now that you will be able vigorously to refute any suggestion of incompetent slackness in your command, you surely will wish me to be recompensed and that can be done by making your authorisation retrospective ... Shall I forward my expenses?'

Salas swore.

'Thank you, Señor. Now as to the facts which prove Colin Short murdered Jiminez and what was his motive for the death of Señorita Coates...'

Fifteen minutes later, Alvarez returned to the dining-room.

'You've been a lifetime!' Dolores said, her voice shrill from worry. 'Are they going to arrest you?'

'Not this time.'

'But that Madrileño was so angry.'

'I persuaded Salas to calm down and

understand it's sensible not to accuse your neighbour of stealing your lamb if you have one of his; also, that there was no need for any hearing to go ahead. Considering everything, I think I've done rather well. I deserve a drink.'

She expressed her relief in typical fashion. 'When a man drinks what he deserves, he has water.'